Murder on the First Date

The Wronged Women's Co-operative: Book 1

T E SCOTT

To all the mums who made it through lockdown without murdering anyone – I salute you!

Prologue

She was not his usual type. There was her age, for a start. And that hair! But Sam Jones had never been one to turn down an easy shag, and this woman would certainly be that.

"This is a nice place," she said, sipping on a large glass of white wine. She had ordered a Chardonnay: he hadn't seen anyone drink that for years. Her hand shook a little as she lifted the glass and he wondered if she had had a few before she left the house.

"It is. Only built five years ago, not that you would know it. A friend of mine handled the planning permission, the council insisted it looked 'olde worlde' for some reason."

"Can't see beyond the end of their nose, the council." The woman gave him a shy smile. She wasn't wrong there.

"Mind you, the food is great," he said, although the steak had been mediocre at best. In truth, he liked the anonymity of the chain pub with its plastic menu and frozen desserts. It was far enough away from his home that there would be no one to recognise him. And even if they did, he was a single guy, nothing wrong with taking a young woman out on a date.

Well, youngish, he thought, catching sight of the tiny wrinkles around the woman's eyes.

"Do you want anything else?"

"No thanks. Maybe you could give me a lift home?"

"Sure." He was a little over the limit, but there was no danger of getting pulled over here. They were half an hour from the nearest town, which in central Scotland was not exactly a metropolis anyway. He missed London. At least the women knew how to dress there. He glanced down at his companion. Were those orthopaedic sandals? Yuck.

He led her to his car. A platinum grey BMW, a few years old now but as immaculate as the day he had bought it. He had it valeted once a month, just to make sure.

He opened the door for her, then got into the driver's seat. He wasn't giving up on the night yet. Perhaps she would be up for a nightcap at his flat, although he didn't normally like bringing women back there. It was so much more difficult to get them to leave in the morning.

"I had a great night," he said, turning his head so that he could look directly into her eyes. They were actually very pretty, dark almond shapes framed with long lashes. She was a bit of a catch after all, he thought, if only she would dress a little better.

"Me too."

When she leaned in for a kiss it took him a little by surprise, but he found he was kissing her back with plenty of enthusiasm. He felt her body press closer and he reached up to the collar of her top. His fingers toyed with a button.

"Hang on," she whispered, pulling back from him. Sam took a breath that was more of a pant.

"Are we going too fast?" he asked with a cheeky grin.

"No, it's just… There's a layby down the road, just after the turn-off for Buckenhill. Why don't we go there? It would be a wee bit more private."

Result! He almost stalled the car as he got into gear and turned out of the car park. He glanced over at the woman but she was staring out of the passenger's window. It just went to show you should never judge a book by its cover. Sensible shoes but a penchant for lay-by sex. Who would have thought it?

When they left the pub car park behind it didn't take long for the road to get dark. It was a cloudy sky with no moon or stars in sight and only the beam of the headlights showed the winding road ahead.

It didn't matter. Since he'd moved up from England three years ago, Sam had driven these roads often enough to know every twist and turn. He drove a little faster than usual, hoping that the woman would enjoy the flip of her stomach as they leapt over each bump in the road.

"Just up here," she called out, and he had to slam on the brakes. He had almost missed the lay-by, but he managed to reverse into it. There were high trees all around them and apart from the dashboard there was total darkness. Perfect.

"I hope you're not scared of the dark," he said, turning to face her. He could just see her profile, lit by the sliver of moon that was trying to poke through the clouds.

"Not at all," she said, and her lips touched his once more. It was all he could do not to rip her clothes off there and then. He ran his hands over her back, searching for an elusive bra strap, just about managing to keep the grin from his face.

And then she raised her hand and he drew back with a gasp. At first he thought she must have caught him with her nails, but the sharp scratch left a throb of pain that didn't go away.

"What are you —"

The last thing he felt was the cool air on his face when she opened the passenger door and disappeared from view.

Chapter 1: Mary

"Did you hear that Mr Jones didn't turn up for school today?"

"No." Mary glanced around the playground, only half listening to Ewan's mum. The woman was a nurse, with a sharp face and an even sharper tongue. Bernie, that was her name, Mary thought, pleased that she had managed to remember. Baby brain made it hard to remember anything, even if her current baby was three years old and trying to eat a potted hydrangea.

"Lauren, put the plant down, honey!" she called out half-heartedly, not expecting her daughter to pay any attention. Which she didn't.

"Apparently the Head was spitting feathers," Bernie continued. She folded her arms across her slim chest. Mary wondered how she had managed to keep her figure. It seemed to her that for most mothers, excess weight gain was as much a part of childbirth as the labour pains. Not for Bernie, however. "It's not the first time he's been too hungover to come in and teach."

"Isn't it?" Mary felt that she should be more outraged, but it was hard to muster the energy. She looked around the playground and did another quick headcount. Yes, four little ginger monsters. None of her children had disappeared yet.

"Oi, Liz!" Bernie waved towards a voluptuous black woman wearing a smart grey suit. The woman waved back and headed in their direction.

"That's wee Sean's mum, isn't it?" Mary asked, adjusting her cardigan so that it covered the stain on her t-shirt. With her perfectly coiled hair and long painted nails, Sean's mum looked like someone out of a courtroom drama, not a school playground.

"Yep. Works in something financial. Pots of money," Bernie said in a whisper before raising her voice. "Did you hear about Mr Jones?"

Liz rolled her eyes. "Drunk again, so I've heard. Tch, shouldn't be allowed. We should make a complaint to the PTA. I'm Liz, by the way."

She gave Mary a dazzling smile.

"Thanks. I'm Mary. Um, is there a PTA?"

"Oh, I forgot you've only just moved," Bernie said. "Yes, there used to be. But the meetings were so long and so boring that nobody was turning up. Now it's just Frances Beatty and the janitor. And even they can't agree on anything."

"Frances Beatty? Whose mum is that?"

"Oh, everyone knows Frances," Bernie laughed, "She's a bit older, her last kid is in primary six now, but she had another three go through the school in the last ten years. Total busybody, more kids than sense, if you know what I mean."

There was an awkward pause.

"Oh well, you know, my four aren't any trouble," Mary said, a blush creeping up from her collarbones.

"I don't mean you, of course, Mary," Bernie said, unabashed. "I mean, you've got mother written all over you."

"Do I?" Mary said, then turned to give a wave to her kids. "I better be getting home anyway."

"How's the house coming on? You've been in what, four months now isn't it?"

"Oh, it's coming along just fine," Mary said, watching in relief as her children started to slouch their way back from the playing field. Each of them had grass stains on every available item of clothing. More washing to do.

"I didn't realise you were Peter's mum," Liz said, her smile disappearing as she spotted Mary's eldest child walking towards them.

"Um, yes, that's him. Come on guys, hurry up!"

"He's in my Sean's class. Quite a wee character isn't he."

"He is that," Mary replied, now trying to gather the kids towards her as quickly as possible. "It's been hard for him moving schools halfway through the year. Hard for them all."

"Why was it you moved again?" Bernie asked.

Mary ducked down to sort out one of the kid's laces that was trailing in the dirt. "My husband's work," she said quickly, the lie that she used so often barely requiring any thought.

"Ah, we should get you out on one of our mum's nights," Liz said, her smile returning. "They're not too debauched, are they Bernie?"

"Not at all."

"Oh, that would be lovely, just text me when you're planning one," Mary said, edging towards the gate before either woman had time to realise that they didn't have her number.

Chapter 2: Mary

Mary strapped Lauren into her car seat, pulled the belt tight and shut the door with a sigh. It wouldn't be until she got home that she allowed herself to relax. Driving a car with four tired children was similar to standing in the centre of a hurricane. Only louder.

"Can we play computer games when we get home?" Peter asked.

"Homework. And no computer games except at weekends. You know that already," Mary said, checking the street was clear of kids before pulling out into the road. A service light had come on the dashboard but she pretended that she couldn't see it.

It was a grey day, the sort of flat, dull light that made the small town look bleak and rundown. In summer, you could believe that the town of Invergryff was like something out of a tourist brochure. There were heather-covered hills in the background and a quaint little town centre full of cafes and hanging baskets. Now that September had passed it had started settling itself in for the winter season, shop shutters stayed down and the streets were already turning sludgy from the fallen leaves. When Mary had bought their new home the sun had made the white render sparkle. Now it looked like something you would find in one of the more liberal prisons.

"Ugh! Peter just poured his water bottle over me!"

"What?" Mary looked in the rear-view mirror and saw that

somehow both Peter and Vikki were soaked through, water all over the back seat. "Oh my god, what happened?"

"We were playing fire engines!" Peter said indignantly.

"Of all the ridiculous…" Mary counted to ten in her head. And then another ten. And another.

Five minutes later they were home, piling out of the car like a localised tornado, dropping bags and pencils and toys as they went. The entire back seat was sopping wet and only Lauren's car seat had survived, thanks to being in the front. It would take hours for the rest of it to dry.

Home. A three bedroom house that felt like a sardine can when they were all there. Two sets of bunkbeds and just enough room to fit in every childish argument you could think of. Mary trudged in after the kids, her arms full of damp, musty smelling clothes.

"Where's your coat, Peter?" she asked as they flung their shoes all over the hall.

"Left it."

"And your PE kit?"

A small shrug.

"Right. Well. Get it tomorrow, okay?" Mary felt the muscle under her eye twitch and she rubbed at it until it stopped. Matt would have given him a right telling off around now. Something about responsibility and how Peter should act his age. Should she do the same? Probably, but Mary was just too tired. She needed to pick her battles. Just until she got back on her feet again. At least she could make them something healthy for dinner, just as soon as she had five minutes to spare.

"Homework!" Mary shouted and helped them get books, pencils, second pencils after one was broken in a fencing battle, rubbers, and rulers. Somehow it was five o'clock. Something quick for dinner then, maybe a nice salad and –

"Crap," Mary whispered, looking at the empty fridge. Nothing to eat unless her kids fancied two strawberry yoghurts and some questionable mayonnaise for dinner. Now I've done it, she thought, I'll have to get them all back in the car and… Damn it, the seats will still be wet! She looked down at the three kids quietly getting on with their homework. The shop was only five minutes' drive, ten minutes to grab a couple of pizzas, five minutes back. Well, she would only be gone twenty minutes. Fifteen if she hustled.

"Okay kids, I've got a wee challenge for you. I've got to nip to the shops. I'll take Lauren with me, but if you are extra specially good you can stay here by yourselves until I get back."

"Dad never let us stay in alone," Vikki said, her eyes narrowed.

"It is character forming. You know, teaching you independence. Important skills for your eventual transition to adulthood," Mary muttered, pulling on her shoes and wiping Lauren's nose at the same time.

"So… I'm in charge then?" Vikki said, chewing on the inside of her lip.

Mary ducked down to her daughter's level. "Well, here's the

thing. Peter should be in charge. But he's…"

"A nightmare," Vikki nodded.

"No! Not at all! Just, well, not suited to a management position. Whereas you…"

"She's a mini Hitler."

"Ah, didn't see you there Peter," Mary felt her face flush. "Sorry about the… I mean, you can be in charge too, it's just…"

"It's okay mum, she's right, I'm a nightmare." Peter shrugged happily. "This whole place would probably burn down with me in charge. Let little Miss Hitler do it."

Mary pinched the bridge of her nose. "Please don't call your sister that. Okay, so Vikki is in charge, but I know that she won't need to bother with you, Peter. You'll just be on the computer, right?"

"I thought we only got game time at the weekend?"

"Just get on the computer, okay? Look, I'm taking Lauren with me, so it'll just be you guys and Johnny to look after. And he'll just watch cartoons and… maybe I should just take all of you after all."

"Are the seats still wet?" Vikki asked.

"Yes. But I could pop a poly bag on them and…"

"We'll be fine," Vikki said, finishing her sums. "Cartoons for me and Johnny and games for Peter. I've got it."

Another flurry of activity and before there was time for second thoughts Mary was out of the house, pulling her youngest child along the drive as quickly as she could.

"Where Vikki gone?" Lauren asked as Mary clipped her into the car seat.

"Your brothers and sister are staying home. We'll just be a few minutes," Mary said, aware that her voice was a few notes higher than usual. Everything was going to be fine, she told herself.

She shut the car door behind her. The blissful silence surrounded her like a warm hug. Ten minutes, she thought. I'll only be ten minutes. She pulled her car keys from her pocket, dislodged a furry raisin from the keyring and turned on the engine.

Chapter 3: Bernie

Bernie took off her glasses so that she could see the guy properly.

"How much did you say it would be?"

"Six hundred, I'm afraid." The garage owner scratched his stomach. He was what, five or six stone overweight, and carrying it all around the middle of his body. Ten years, max, Bernie thought, before all that cholesterol would clog up his arteries to the critical level. Heart attack waiting to happen. Served him right, the old crook.

"That seems like a lot."

"Well, it's the price of parts at the moment. And the labour, of course."

"What did you say it was again?"

"The brake pads are totally worn through. And it's a Renault so, you know. French."

"Right." Bernie took out her phone, put her glasses back on and tapped something into the screen. "Strange as it looks like the average cost for this type of car is around two hundred and fifty."

The man flinched. "Aye, well, yours are in an awkward position, see?"

"I see. Tell me what, why don't you take another look at your invoice before I write up my review for you online. And send it to the local social media pages, telling them exactly what you charged me, okay?"

"I guess I could double-check," he grumbled.

"You do that. I'll be back in an hour."

Bernie strode out of the garage and resisted the temptation to look back to see if the owner was pulling faces behind her back. He'd probably still overcharge her, but at least he would ask for something a bit more sensible. If she didn't need the car for work she would have pushed him even harder. What a prick.

Her work phone rang.

"Lucy here. How long are you going to be? Mrs Peterson is kicking off about her blood pressure. Again."

"Harry can do it, surely?"

"'Course he can, but will she let 'a man' into her room? She said he would be looking up her 'drawers'. She's a hoot!"

Bernie laughed. "I'll be there as soon as the car's fixed. How's Mrs McGillivray?"

Lucy's voice turned serious. "Not much better I'm afraid. Barely eaten. I even took in some chocolates, Milk Tray, you know, the fudge ones? She hardly touched them."

"Damn. Listen, I'm going to grab a coffee, then I'll see if the car's done. Be there as soon as I can." Bernie ended the call, and then stood still in the street for a few seconds. Well, it wasn't like it was unexpected. Annie McGillivray was ninety-eight with sciatica, high blood pressure, a heart murmur and only one working eye. And, of course, they didn't have favourites at the Campsie Glen Nursing Home. But if they did, Annie would have been everyone's favourite. Sharp as a tack with stories about every person she had ever met, she was the life and soul of the home. Every bingo night, every yoga class she'd be right in the thick of it, laughing her tits off.

Bernie sniffed. Ah well, there were worse ways to go. She had seen a few, especially when she worked in A and E over in Glasgow. Much better to go peacefully in bed nearing a century of life than to be stabbed by some wannabe gangster outside a nightclub as a kid, that was for sure.

The loud wail of sirens came from behind her and Bernie turned to watch as they raced along the main street. Two police cars and an ambulance. Out of habit, she thought through the possibilities. Road accident maybe? Although no fire engine. Another police car passed, this one a grey saloon with lights in the grill. CID? She had watched enough police dramas to know that would be the detectives. So not your average petty crime. Interesting.

She took out her phone and checked the local social media groups. Nothing on them yet, and they were generally quicker than the news. Mind you, there was someone she could ask. Time to get to work.

Chapter 4: Liz

Liz had dropped Sean off at his grandmother's to get some studying done, but now that she had the time to herself she couldn't concentrate. She had turned her phone on silent, but she could still see the screen light up every time an email came through. Work, of course, and she didn't need to open the mail to see who it would be from.

She pushed her phone down into her pocket and drove to her favourite café. A chain, one of half a dozen that had popped up around the town. Every place exactly the same from the type of brew on offer to the faux leather seating. Reliable and safe, just like she liked it.

Growing up, her parents had been tea drinkers, something that had helped them integrate with their Scottish friends when they had arrived from Nigeria thirty years ago. In an act of uncharacteristic rebellion, Liz had discovered coffee when she went to university and now she didn't drink anything else. An Americano in the morning, with an extra shot if she was feeling particularly tired, set her up for the day.

Dave – wonderful, reliable Dave – considered her coffee habit a wanton extravagance. Of course, he couldn't say anything about it as she was the one who brought in the majority of the money. But she knew he didn't approve. She sipped from her takeaway cup, the dark smoky liquid threatening to burn her tongue, and smiled.

Liz put the cup into the central console of her Audi and pulled away from the café. Her work phone vibrated in her pocket, but she didn't pick it up. She had flexitime agreed at the corporate level, but that didn't mean there wasn't plenty of resentment when she used an afternoon to study or pick up Sean. She would have to answer the calls when she got to the library, but there was no rush. She could take the long way there.

The long route took her through a succession of 1960s housing estates. They were almost indistinguishable from the one Liz had grown up in. Not poor, but certainly not rich. The sort of place where curtains twitched if you didn't put out your bins on time. Growing up, Liz had found them stifling, parochial, with the sort of low level racism that was easier to ignore than forgive. Now that she was older she could appreciate the sense of community, the comforting sight of groups of kids playing on street corners.

Kids just like – crap!

Liz spun the wheel to the right and gasped as her head whipped from one side to the other. Her white SUV mounted the curb and smashed into a yellow grit bin. Luckily she had only been crawling along but she felt the juddering impact right up her spine.

She puffed out a breath, then opened her door and staggered out of the car.

"What. The. F –" She looked around to see a group of tiny, wide-eyed faces staring up at her.

"Um. Okay." Liz bit down on the swear words she had been just about to blurt out. "What just happened? There was a kid in the road. I think he was… was there a vacuum cleaner?" Liz rubbed at her temples. There was no one in the road, just a row of nervous kids standing on the pavement. Had she imagined the whole thing?

"I was trying to see if it could suck up snails," a small voice said. Liz peered through the group of kids to see a boy with ginger hair that she knew she should recognise.

"It's… aren't you Peter?" Sensing that there was a row coming, the rest of the kids disappeared, apart from Peter and his red-headed siblings.

"Yes, Miss."

"It's Liz. Sean's mum. You don't have to call me Miss, I'm not a teacher."

"Look a bit like a teacher," Peter sniffed. "You have teacher shoes."

"No, I… never mind that. What the hell were you doing playing in the road?"

"The snails, Miss."

The boy didn't seem to have a scratch on him, but he must have been only a few inches away from her wheel. If she hadn't moved quickly enough… It didn't bear thinking about.

"Right, you said. Okay, first things first, let's get you guys back home. Which one is your house?"

"We can get back by ourselves," Peter said. His neck was red and Liz could see he had started to realise that there might be serious consequences on the horizon.

"I don't think so. I want a chat with your mum."

"She's… she's not in." The girl sniffed and wiped at her eyes. Liz thought it must have given Peter's sister a proper fright when she saw the car crash. The youngest son didn't look too bothered: he was picking up the crystals of plexiglass that were scattered over the pavement and putting them in his pocket.

"What do you mean, she's not in?"

"She went to the shops."

Liz narrowed her eyes. "And your little brother is what, primary one?"

"He's seven. We were meant to stay in the house. Only Pete wanted to go outside and I wasn't to leave him alone and…"

The girl started to wail. Liz patted her on the arm. She had never been much good at comforting crying children. Sean had learned to comfort himself before he was out of nappies.

"Right. I think we'll get you all back in the house and we'll wait for your mum."

"You won't tell, will you?" Peter asked hopefully.

"Of course I'm going to tell. But it's not just you guys that I'm going to have some serious words with."

Even Peter's head was hanging low by now. What was it Sean had said about him? Hadn't he been the one that had flooded the toilets on his first day and called it a climate change protest? Liz was pretty sure that had been Peter.

Just as Liz was about to lead them into the house, a battered estate car pulled into the street, then slammed to a halt. The person behind the wheel looked vaguely familiar. It was only then that Liz realised she had been talking to her after school. Bernie's friend, wasn't it Mary something? Well, it wouldn't stop her giving the woman a piece of her mind.

Mary got out of the car. Her face was ashen and her mouth was a perfect circle. She clapped her hands to her cheeks. "Five minutes!" she screamed. "I was only gone for five minutes!"

"It's okay," Liz found herself saying. "It was just…"

The woman was shaking all over. "I can't… What happened? Are they all right? Look at your car!"

"It's not as bad as it looks," Liz managed. The woman's terror was unsettling her. She had intended to tell her off for leaving the kids home alone, but at this moment it would have been simply cruel. Like kicking a tiny, feeble kitten.

Mary grabbed her children toward her and spun them around, checking for injuries.

"They're fine, honestly. I swerved in time…"

"You mean they were in the road?"

Liz wondered if the woman was going to be sick.

"Yes. With a vacuum cleaner. Look, can we go inside."

"Of course." Now that she had checked the kids over the colour was starting to return to Mary's cheeks. "It's that house right there, with the blue door. Would you mind taking them in while I get Lauren from the car?"

Liz hadn't even noticed the youngest child who had begun to wail in her car seat.

"Sure. I'll put the kettle on."

Chapter 5: Liz

It had been years since Liz had drunk a cup of proper Scottish tea. Even at her parents' house she had managed to sneak in a jar of instant coffee for when she visited.

"Two sugars for me, please," Mary said, hovering around in the background. Two sugars! It was just like being back at her mum's. Liz looked down at the sugar pot. What the hell. She added two to her own cup as well.

"I'm sorry about the state of the kitchen," Mary said, her voice still trembling. "I haven't had a chance to tidy yet today."

Or this week, Liz thought. The house was small, a galley kitchen with a dining room off it that barely had room for a table. On their way to the kitchen they had passed a tiny living room full of plastic toys.

"It's fine, really."

Mary hadn't stopped apologising since they'd walked through the front door. First, for Peter and his antics in the road, for the state of Liz's car, for the general disrepair of the house... At first, Liz had felt sorry for her, but now she was just finding it irritating.

"How long did the car recovery guy say he'd be?" Mary chewed on her thumbnail.

"An hour or so." They closed the door of the dining room to get some respite from the children who seemed to be fighting the battle of Bannockburn over the sofa cushions.

Mary blew on her tea. She was very pretty, Liz thought, now that she got a chance to look at the woman. Her blond hair needed dyed, but even with the roots showing and a stained cardigan, she would have turned heads.

"I guess they got their hair from their dad," Liz said, trying to fill the silence.

"Yes, he's the ginger." Mary's back stiffened and she looked down at the floor.

"Working, is he?"

"He's away a lot. Works on the rigs."

"In Aberdeen?"

"Most of the time. Sometimes in the Middle East."

"Why did you move down here then? I mean, it's not as handy for Aberdeen."

Mary still didn't look up. "Ah, well, you get a lot more for your money down here. And my mum's just outside Glasgow so... It made sense."

There was a story there, Liz thought. No way would someone who worked in Aberdeen want to live down in the central belt. Pity Mary didn't want to say what was actually going on. He's probably left her high and dry with the kids. Wouldn't be the first or last guy to do that.

"And the kids have settled in fine?"

"Apart from Peter. I get a phone call from the office at least once a week. And now playing in the road! Honestly, I'm so sorry about –"

"I said don't worry about it. I mean, I'll admit when they said they were home alone I was a bit… surprised."

Mary groaned and squeezed her arms across her chest. "I know, I'm an idiot. I would totally understand if you reported me for it. I never used to do things like that. Only I needed some food for dinner and I just thought, well, I guess I wasn't thinking. I swear, it won't happen again."

Liz took a tiny sip of the sugary tea. Then another. It was better than she remembered. "You know, my mum worked every hour she could when I was growing up. I was a latchkey kid, back in the day. I guess I understand why you did it, even though it's not really the done thing now. You were desperate, right?"

"Right."

They lapsed into silence, only broken by the muffled shouts that came through the wall.

"What did you do before you were married?" Liz asked.

"I was a biologist." Mary caught Liz's baffled face and laughed. "I know, hard to believe it now, but I used to have a half-decent brain. Graduated in biology, took a job with SEPA, looking at the impact of industry on the environment. Wrote a lot of very boring reports. Did that for four years before I got pregnant with Peter. Then Vikki followed soon after, then the other two and well, I never went back."

"Biologist," Liz rubbed her chin. "Now that is interesting. Have you thought about going back to work?"

"Can't afford the childcare. Hopefully when Lauren is in school I can get something. I'd love to work, but honestly, it's just not feasible at the moment."

Liz leaned forward, the hot tea still sweet on her tongue. "Perhaps I can help you with that."

Chapter 6: Bernie

Bernie checked her watch. Eighteen minutes since she'd been on shift and already three minor catastrophes and one major one. The nursing home was short staffed as usual, and they had just had an intake of three new service users. Two women and one man, all in their eighties with complex needs and even more complex paperwork.

"Not much chance of getting a break tonight," a young cleaner called Lynn said as she hurried past the office carrying bedlinen.

"I'll make a cuppa in half an hour, you want one?"

"Always."

It was a cliché, but the whole place really did run on tea. And the occasional biscuit, especially if it was a chocolate one. Not that Bernie ate biscuits. Since her 'Incredible Weight Loss Journey' as the local paper had termed it, she had been strict on her sugar intake. She wasn't about to fall back into old habits for the sake of a single bourbon.

There, done. The paperwork was filled in and she could pull her eyes away from the computer screen to do her rounds. But just as she was about the leave, the office door banged open.

"I have had it with that man!" Lucy Dubanowski slammed the door behind her. She was nearly fifty now and had been living in Scotland so long that her accent had retained barely any trace of the small town in Poland she had left as a teenager.

Didn't stop the less politically correct patients from making comments about the Eastern Europeans taking everyone's jobs. To which Bernie always countered, well, clearly the Scottish folk don't like dealing with your nonsense and that normally shut them up.

"Let me guess, was it Mr Barry?"

"Aye, the old misery guts. Won't take the new pills even though the Doctor explained exactly why he has to have them. Accused me of poisoning him!"

"Chance would be a fine thing," Bernie laughed. "He's not got dementia, does he?"

"Not at all. Sharp as a tack. Just bloody miserable. I'm sure he was trying to look down my shirt as well. God help me but I'd rather spend an hour cleaning the loos than trying to get him to take a single bloody statin. No wonder his kids never visit."

"Aye well, you know that that doesn't mean anything. Some of the meanest old buggers have children who come every Sunday, regular as anything."

"Waiting for the inheritance most likely."

"Lucy!"

"Sorry. I'm just in a bad mood today. You all right to take over?"

"Of course. You go get your head down."

Lucy trudged out of the room and Bernie made a mental note

to have a stern word with Mr Barry. He had been a policeman before he retired, used to giving orders rather than receiving them, no doubt. Life in a care home didn't suit everyone, but there was no need to take it out on her staff. Maybe she would sign him up for the weekly Bingo, or would that count as a cruel and unusual punishment? Her mouth curled into a grin. It might be worth it to see the look on his face.

She checked her watch. Yes, just enough time to pop in to see her favourite patient before general rounds.

Annie McGillivray had a corner room with windows on two sides. It always smelled of her brand of face powder and lavender talcum powder. When Bernie went in, Annie was sitting in the armchair by the window, her eyes shut and her mouth slightly open. The Guardian was on her knee, a half-completed crossword folded carefully on the top.

"Afternoon Annie," Bernie called out from the doorway.

"Oh, it's yourself." Annie straightened up in her chair and took out a handkerchief to wipe her watery eyes.

"Fancy a tea?" Bernie asked.

"I'd rather have a brandy. The bottle's in the cupboard over there."

Bernie frowned. "It's not five o'clock yet. Isn't it a wee bit early?"

"Are you the nurse or the nanny, girl?"

"Sorry, Annie," Bernie smiled and poured a generous measure into the glass that never left the bedside table. "I heard you've been off your food."

"You make me sound like a naughty puppy. I just wasn't hungry today."

"Mmn. You'll take some dinner then?"

"Of course."

Bernie knew not to push it. Annie had her marbles still firmly gripped and she did not appreciate any suggestion of weakness. A young girl went past with a trolley and she grabbed a tea, noting that Annie had hidden her glass behind the curtains.

"I hear that Graeme Barry has been giving our Lucy some grief again," Annie said once the trolley had continued its squeaky progress up the hall.

"Won't take his medicine."

"Well, I'll have a word. I remember him as a young lad. Happier with his fists than his letters, that's for sure. Police work suited him down to the ground, and like a lot of them he never took to retirement. His wife was a lovely lass, but when she died he lost any joy in himself. Yes, I'll have a word all right. Tell him just what his wee Millie would have thought about his attitude."

Annie's eyes flickered to the window. Annie's room overlooked the care home car park, and a little further on, the general hospital. If you positioned your armchair in the window just right, you could see right up to the automatic doors that led to A and E.

Bernie gulped down her tea. Nearly time for rounds. "Did you see the ambulances pass by earlier?"

"Aye, and one went back into the hospital without its lights on. Straight into the emergency bay, but not rushing. Know what that means?"

"No."

"That the poor soul was already dead. Body covered on the stretcher too, so not a pretty sight."

"Now that is interesting. Wonder who it could be?"

"Hopefully some old lush that died peacefully in his sleep. That's what I'm hoping for. Dreaming of Gary Cooper if I'm lucky."

"Never heard of him. Was he a singer?"

"An actor. Drop dead gorgeous, he was. The most beautiful set of lips I've ever seen. And an arse you could bounce pennies off."

Bernie nearly spat out her tea. "You are a wicked old besom, aren't you?"

"Got to be. Wickedness and brandy are the only things keeping me going. Secret to a long life, that is."

"Don't think the Doctors would agree with you," Bernie said, taking the empty glass and replacing it on the bedside table.

"Think they know everything, don't they? Only, human beings are more than a collection of blood and organs and they would do well to remember it. Take our dead body, just arrived at the hospital. Give it twenty-four hours and I'll be able to tell you all about it."

"I'm counting on it, Annie," Bernie said and she left to do her rounds.

Chapter 7: Walker

When the CID car pulled up, Constable Owen Walker turned off his personal mobile and secured it away in a pouch in his jacket. Technically he shouldn't have it on him at all, but like all the other guys, he couldn't resist checking his phone every once in a while. The PDA supplied by Police Scotland was fine and everything, but you couldn't check your score on Dungeon Tamers Online with it.

It had been three years since he had marched out of the training college in Tulliallan in his new uniform and a sense that from now on, anything could happen. He had spent most of his probation in the capital and had only been in Renfrewshire for a month. Walker already missed Edinburgh more than he thought possible. Yes, it was busy in the city, and half the time you went home covered in someone else's bodily fluids, but at least it was never boring.

Apart from regular callers – the sort of poor souls that never made it onto the news, even when something really bad happened to them – there wasn't that much to do when he was on shift. Patrol, show face… that was pretty much it. And yes, it could get rowdy on a Friday night, but hardly like it did in the capital city where local druggies met posh English students trying to negotiate the back streets of Leith. Nothing like that ever happened around here.

That was why when he had first seen the car, he had driven past it. After all, it wasn't that unusual for someone to stop in a layby. It was quite a picturesque part of the world, even if it was lacking the grandeur of the mountains up north. Plenty of challenging walks for people that found that sort of thing interesting. Ramblers and the like. Not the sort of people that usually troubled Walker on his shifts.

He had driven past, absently noting the make and model of the car, before something poked at his brain. Had the passenger door been left open? He drove on another mile before he decided that it definitely had. He turned around at a local farm track and drove back to the layby.

His spidey senses were tingling before his boots hit the ground. The passenger door was open and there was no path leading anywhere, just furrowed fields on all sides. No reason for anyone to leave a car here. He had just reached for the radio when a flash of movement caught his eye. A single fat blue bottle flew out of the open door.

Moving quickly now, Walker ran around to the driver's side to see – yes – a body in the front seat. A man, maybe in his thirties, with his head resting on the steering wheel. Caucasian with dark brown hair and a silky navy shirt and jeans. Clearly dead, although Walker opened the door and checked his pulse anyway, just in case. Then he phoned it in to the station.

And now it was the next morning, CID were here and he had to look sharp. If he was lucky they might even let him be involved in the case, and that could be his first step out of the Shire. On the path to… well, hopefully not Mordor, but maybe a fast track to his Sergeant's exams. And a move to somewhere a little less dull.

"You were first on the scene, weren't you? What's your name again?" The man over from the Glasgow headquarters had introduced himself as Detective Inspector Rob Macleod, with a teuchter accent you could have cut glass with.

"Yes sir. It's Constable Walker. I noticed the vehicle at sixteen hundred hours and went to take a look."

"Gloves?"

"Of course," Walker bristled. He was hardly new to the job. "I touched the door handle and then the victim's neck to take a pulse which was negative."

"I'd have said so. According to the pathologist he'd been dead for at least twelve hours by then."

"I followed procedure."

Macleod moved his neck in what might have been a nod or just a twitch. Walker kept silent. If the guy was determined to throw his weight around he wasn't going to be the one to get in the Inspector's way.

Walker watched as Macleod looked around the car. The body was long gone, lying in the morgue until it was time for the post-mortem. Forensics had been and gone too, poking around with their tweezers and plastic bags, taking anything that looked interesting or out of place back to the laboratory for analysis.

He wished he'd had time to grab a coffee. Walker hadn't gone to bed until two and then it was up again at six so that he could be one of the first ones in the office. There were two other constables on shift, both more experienced than him but his eagerness had paid off as Sergeant Paul O'Connor had spotted him and sent him back to the crime scene.

"Talk me through what you saw," Macleod said as he examined the ground around the layby.

"As I said, I checked the pulse, then called for backup. I then made a visual examination of the deceased."

"And what did you see?"

"Male, aged thirty to forty. Expensive clothes, the jeans were a designer brand. No visible injuries."

"Interesting, isn't it? Could be a heart attack, but he's a bit young. What made you think it might be foul play?"

"The passenger door was open, suggesting that there had been someone sitting there when they were in the layby."

Macleod nodded. "Good. Anything else?"

"A slight smell of perfume on the passenger seat. I noted it in the file."

The DI ducked into the car and gave the seat a sniff. "Nearly gone now, but I think you're right. Difficult to prove it was from the other night though. Think you'd know it again?"

"Possibly," Walker replied.

Macleod scratched his temple. He had thin blond hair that was already receding. It made him look older, although Walker thought he was probably under fifty.

"It's the cup final this weekend."

"Are you a Rangers supporter?" Walker asked, then instantly regretted it when he saw the other man's face.

"Can't stand bloody football. No, I just meant that we're even more short staffed than usual. You seem a capable lad. Fancy a stint on the Major Investigation Team?"

Walker couldn't keep the grin from his face.

"Yes sir," he said.

Chapter 8: Mary

When she woke up on Saturday morning the first thing Mary thought of was the smashed up car and her children's frightened faces. Liz had been incredibly kind not to report her to the social work, or the police even. She could have been judged an unfit mother, had her children taken away. She pushed her face into the pillow. How had it come to this? Just a few months ago she had been like any other yummy mummy, sitting in her delightful five bed new build, reading Good Housekeeping and thinking about investing in an air fryer. Now she was the sort of mum that would feature in the tabloid press with smudged mascara and a dressing gown on, yelling at the Social for taking her kids away.

Poor, that was what she was. The kind of poverty that she had never dreamed of. She had barely used her credit card up in Aberdeen, now she was almost at the limit. Next month she would have to ask her parents for a loan or the kids would have nothing to eat. It was humiliating.

Matt would give her money, eventually. Child support, that was what it was called. She would have to sort it out soon. It was just that going down that route meant that everything truly was over.

Mary forced her body out of bed and pulled on some clothes. As if moving down here hadn't meant their relationship was finished. Had part of her thought he would ask her to come back? Probably. Well, that hadn't happened and now she had to face facts. This was her life, and the life she had chosen for her kids. It was up to her to make it better.

Funny to think it was Liz that had given her the tiniest spark of hope. The job was only a few hours a week, taking minutes, basic administrative work. Well below what she was used to, but it could be done in the evenings. Would Mary be interested in something like that?

Of course she blooming well was! It wouldn't pay much money, but it would keep the wolf from the door, not to mention the tiger, the shark and the herd of bloody elephants too. Only thing was, Liz was kind of cagey about who she would be working for. A co-operative, she said, and Mary hadn't managed to get any more information than that. She just hoped it wouldn't be anything illegal.

"Can I have another slice of toast?" Vikki asked, and Mary calculated how much of the loaf was left.

"Of course you can," she said, putting a single slice in the toaster. There was just enough bread left for breakfast for the kids tomorrow. She would just have bran flakes instead.

Mary held the cool milk bottle up to her pounding temple. Even if it is illegal, she thought, I'll take the damn job. I don't have any other choice.

Chapter 9: Bernie

"I prefer the doughnuts with the sugar on the top. The jam ones are too sickly." Mrs Battaglia licked a spot of raspberry jam from her upper lip.

"I'll remember that for next time," Bernie said, checking her watch. She could take an hour for her break, of course, but she never did. If she was away from the home for more than thirty minutes everything started to fall apart.

"You brought the rolls too? And the meat slices"

"Yes, yes, it's all there."

"Thank you. My boys will be very happy."

Mrs Battaglia's boys were in their twenties now but still living at home. It meant that her cleaning job didn't stretch very far when it came to feeding the family. Bernie was happy to help out, especially when she got a little something in return.

"I heard that someone died yesterday."

"No, I don't think so," the cleaner shook her head. Bernie was about to object when the older woman held up her index finger. "I think maybe they died the day before. They just found the body yesterday."

"Is that so?" Bernie raised her eyebrows.

"Yes, that was what they were saying at the station." When Mrs Battaglia had started cleaning at the home, she had impressed Bernie with her work ethic and her ability to put up with the most difficult of the patients. When she had discovered that the woman also worked part time at the police station, it had been too good an opportunity to pass up.

"Have they said who it is yet?"

The cleaner paused. "They did. But, I am not sure I should tell you. This is not someone's husband getting a speeding ticket. This is a dead body. I could get in big, big trouble for this."

Bernie's eyes narrowed. "You know you can trust me."

"I know. But still, it is too risky."

There was a pause while the cleaner carefully wiped her face with a disposable napkin.

"All right," Bernie said slowly. "What if I could go to M&S tomorrow? Pick up a couple of bottles of decent plonk? Would that go down well with the boys?"

"Make it two cases of beer. My boys like beer."

"Fine."

"The name has not been officially released yet. They are waiting for the identification, I think. But they all know who it is."

"Well, spit it out!"

"It's that teacher. The new one. Mr Jones."

Bernie hissed in a breath. Mr Jones! The handsome but feckless primary school teacher! Now that was interesting.

She stood up to leave. This was something far juicier than any doughnut.

Chapter 10: Liz

Liz spooned some steaming red jollof rice onto her son's plate.

"Can't we have pizza?"

She gave Sean her best stern glare. "Nanny is here tonight, so we're having jollof rice."

"She'll only moan that you didn't use her recipe."

"I know."

The doorbell rang and Liz hurried to let her parents in.

"Sorry we're late. Your father was doing something on his computer." Liz's mum rushed past with a quick, perfumed hug for her daughter. "Where's my little angel?"

"Nanny!" Sean wrapped his arms around his grandmother. Liz still found it strange that her mother, the formidable Mrs Grace Okoro who had worked like a demon every hour of God's day, and who Liz had been more than a little afraid of as a child, had somehow become Nanny. An indulgent, generous grandparent with a softness that hadn't existed with her own daughter.

"Dinner's ready."

"Great. Starving." Liz's dad, John, was a man of few words. He ruffled his grandson's hair then sat down at the table."

"Jollof rice with chicken and plenty of coleslaw, just how you like it, dad."

He gave her a thumbs up.

"Is there spinach in this?" Nanny gave the rice an exploratory poke, like a doctor performing a particularly gruesome colonoscopy.

"A little. I thought it would up the veg content for Sean."

"I never put spinach in mine."

"I know, mum."

Liz's phone buzzed and she flinched.

"Would that be your boss texting you?" Nanny's thick black eyebrows settled into the frown that always made Liz feel like a naughty teenager. "On a Saturday?"

"No, it's probably just Bernie, asking what time I'm heading around," Liz lied. Bernie hardly ever bothered to text, she preferred to catch up face to face. It would be work, of course, she didn't need to look at her screen to see that.

"You work too hard," Nanny said as if Liz hadn't spoken. "Where's that husband of yours anyway?"

"Dave's at a sales conference in London this week. I told you that, didn't I?"

"I suppose you did. Why do opticians need sales conferences anyway?"

"Don't ask me," Liz said, trying to keep her tone light.

"An excuse for a boys weekend, most likely."

"Well, he deserves one, doesn't he? He works hard."

"Huh. Not as hard as you do. I hope he remembers that you paid for this house."

Liz opened her mouth to reply when her dad stood up.

"Football?" John pointed at the garden and Sean jumped out of his seat.

"Just for half an hour," Liz said, taking Sean's plate. "You've still to have a bath before bedtime."

"We can give him his bath if you want to get away earlier," Grace said and Liz felt a wave of gratitude wash away the usual resentment.

"Thanks mum, that would be great."

"What are you doing at your book group tonight?"

"Oh, the new Richard Osman."

Liz picked up the plates and put them in the dishwasher, noting that her mother had cleared her plate of jollof rice despite the spinach.

"Didn't you do that last week?"

Crap. Liz was finding it difficult to remember the lies. "Well… it's a long book and we had a lot to say."

"More interested in wine and gossiping, I'll bet."

"There's a bit of that too."

Her mother took a dishcloth and started to wipe down the table. "I'm glad you've found this group of mums, you know. You need to have a social life outside work."

"I've got Dave," Liz countered.

"Ach, husbands, they don't count. Look at your dad. Forty years married and he spends most of his evenings in the study, tapping away on his computer."

"Really? He never even wanted a smartphone. What's he doing on the computer?"

"Oh, I don't know, he's always on the internet. Sometimes I wonder if he is talking to women on there."

"Dad? I don't think you have to worry about that."

Her mum laughed. "Not unless he finds a woman that can cook better than me. I'm not worried about your dad, I'm just making the point that you need a life outside your marriage."

"I'm not sure if a book group counts as a life, but I'll take it on board."

"Will you be late tonight?"

"Shouldn't think so. Thanks again for babysitting."

"You know it's no trouble. I've brought my latest true crime to read. This one is about a man who chops up women and keeps them in a chest freezer. Right down the bottom with the frozen chicken."

"Lovely. See you later."

Chapter 11: Bernie

Bernie watched her husband, Finn, take his boots off at the front door, next to the bag of tools that he never left in the van, just in case.

"Any tea left?"

She leaned towards him so he could give her a quick, stubbly kiss.

"Yes. Just a pasta thing, but there's plenty still in the pan. And broccoli too."

"Yuk," Finn said, making an exaggerated disgusted face.

"You're worse than your son! Eat your greens."

"Yes, dear. Ewan in his room?"

"Aye. He's had his dinner, he's just playing computer games for a bit. You've only to put him to bed in an hour or so."

"Your ladies and wine night is tonight, isn't it?"

"Actually, we mostly drink gin now."

Finn snorted. "If you say so. Going to be gossiping about how rubbish all your husbands are, as usual?"

Bernie carefully ironed the collar of her work uniform. "It may surprise you to learn that we barely talk about you at all."

"I'm sure. Listen, have you washed my coat?"

"It's hanging up on the back of the door to dry. How did it get so filthy?"

"It's this job over at the school. Them gutters haven't been cleaned for years, no wonder they're all cracked. Anyway, the apprentice stuck the jet wash hose in one end and it came out all over my coat. The lads were hooting with laughter."

"I bet, it's not them that do your washing."

"Ach, he bought me a pint to make up for it."

"Are you working tomorrow too?"

"Yes, got a homer on just around the corner. Should be an early finish though."

Bernie shrugged. It was never an early finish, never mind what he said.

"I'm okay to pop out tonight though?"

"Sure. I'll just have a quiet beer to myself then head off to bed."

Bernie looked down at the pile of ironing, all warm and neat. One beer was never enough though, was it, Finn? One beer led to another, which led to six or seven empty cans in the bin the next day. Not so bad, if it was just at the weekend, only lately it had been happening on week nights too.

If Ewan starts noticing I'll do something about it, Bernie told herself. I'll have to then, God help me. It was a good marriage, all things considered. They barely ever fought, and he would never raise a hand to her. But Bernie knew well enough the number of relationships that could fall apart with never a harsh word spoken. The love that could slip through the cracks.

She pulled on her coat.

"Will you be late?" Finn asked, cracking the ring pull on his can.

"Yes, I think I will."

Chapter 12: Liz

Liz arrived first and grabbed the key from under the flower pot. She juggled her Marks bag in one hand while she unlocked the door. It had been an absolute godsend when Annie McGillivray had said they could use her house to meet up. In the first few weeks of their not-quite-book-group, they had met at Bernie's, but they were always mindful of her husband and son in the other room. Annie had wanted someone to keep an eye on her house while she was in the nursing home, so it was a win-win.

The décor was a perfect example of a magazine interior, but that magazine was from 1978 and it had never been changed since. Liz put her bag of supplies down on the formica dining room table and began to set out the drinks and snacks.

The doorbell rang and she answered it to see Bernie and a very nervous-looking Mary.

"She nearly didn't come," Bernie said, ushering the younger woman in front of her.

"I was just worried about leaving the kids, that's all. But Bernie sorted someone for me."

"Who?" Liz asked, showing Mary into the dining room and pressing a drink into her hand.

"I sent one of the N's over."

"The N's?" Mary asked.

"Nieces and nephews," Liz explained, "Bernie is the youngest of six children. She has more than a dozen adult nieces and nephews and none of us can tell them apart."

"Oi!" A voice called from the front door.

"Apart from Alice, who is, of course, the favourite."

"Damn right," Alice replied, walking into the room and giving Bernie a kiss. She was in denim overalls tonight, with a lace top underneath. The sort of outfit that you can only pull off when you're under twenty-five.

"Anyway, Auntie Bernie just calls us the N's for short," Alice said, slouching into one of the dining chairs. "It does make life easier. Who is it that's babysitting for you?"

"Jackie."

"Ah, she'll be grand. Jackie's got two of her own. She loves kids. She'll not do you wrong."

"Good to know," Mary said.

Liz poured a glass of water for Alice, straight from the tap. Bernie's niece was one of these strange young women who didn't drink. Dark, bobbed hair, stick thin with a nose piercing, she would probably have been called a goth when Liz was growing up. Now she had no idea what that sort of twenty-year-old called themselves, and she would have felt ancient if she'd asked.

"Ooh, scones!" Mary reached out a hand only to hear a discreet cough beside her.

"We don't eat until after we've finished business," Bernie said sternly.

Mary pulled her hand back. "And, if you don't mind me asking, what exactly is this business?"

"What did Liz tell you?"

"Not much. Well, practically nothing in fact. Don't get me wrong, I'm pleased that you have invited me, but I can't take a job until I know what I'd be doing."

"Well, we're not a book group, that's for sure," Liz gave her a broad smile. "I guess we are a sort of private consultancy. We help people with legal problems."

"Nah, we fight crime!" Alice said, bouncing in her seat. "It's like three Jessica Fletchers, and I'm their plucky sidekick."

Liz winced at the idea that she was in the same age category as Angela Lansbury. "Surely you're a bit old for Murder She Wrote?"

Alice rolled her eyes. "Saw it on streaming, didn't I?"

"Sorry, I still don't understand…"

Bernie put down her glass. "We're a private investigation agency, although we don't use those terms. We call ourselves the Wronged Women's Co-operative."

"WWC for short."

"Catchy," Mary said, her eyes wide.

"Why don't I get us a round of gins and you can explain,

Bernie," Liz said, carefully placing herself between Mary and the door just in case the woman decided to bolt.

"All right. Make it a double this time, I'm not driving home."

Chapter 13: Mary

Mary was on her second large gin, but it wasn't the alcohol making her feel dizzy.

"You're trying to tell me that you're private investigators? Like something off a TV show?"

"I don't think they put middle-aged women on TV, do they?" Bernie said. The nurse seemed to be in her element, sitting at the head of the table and giving out orders. "Alice, no scones for me, would you pass me over my rice cakes? No, I'm not sure there's a name for what Liz and I do. Consultants is a good one, if a little vague. We help people."

"Wronged women? Wasn't that what you said?" Like something out of a Jane Austen novel, Mary thought, but didn't add.

"I know what you're thinking: it's all a bit of a joke, right? And that's how it started." Bernie tore a rice cake into tiny pieces and started crunching them down. "Well, actually it started with the Pride of the Clyde."

Now Mary was lost again. "Sorry, the what?"

"The Pride of the Clyde. A twenty-foot sailboat. A yacht, by any other name. Was it four engines the thing had?"

"Six, I believe," Liz said.

"I'm sorry, I still don't follow."

Bernie puffed out a sigh. "Of course you don't, we haven't explained yet. You see, it was Elly Maclean that told us about her husband. Ex-husband, as he is now. Anyway, he ran off with a yoga instructor. Can you imagine? Apparently she was very flexible, if you know what I mean. Well, I knew Elly because her old mum was in the nursing home, and she knew I was good at finding things out. And the lawyers were umming and ahhing during the divorce negotiations and none of them knew about the yacht. But Elly had heard a rumour that there was this boat over at St Andrews and that's where all the money had gone. He'd been planning it for months, the git, long before he asked for a divorce. Squirrelling the money away through a series of bank accounts that she didn't have access to. Well, it's not exactly my area, but I remembered that I knew someone who worked in finance."

Liz took a mock bow. "That would be me! When Bernie told me about the yacht, I did my best to help, and I had some friends that knew how these sorts of hidden funds worked. We traced the yacht, found out where the mooring fees were going and bingo! The problem was we still couldn't prove it was his."

"So Bernie asked me to go over and take some photos," Alice took up the story. "I'm studying photography for my HNC. I've got a decent long distance lens so I got some blinders, with the snake and his new girlfriend wandering about in a bikini. I mean, it was Scotland in June, she must have been freezing!"

"Well, between Bernie, Alice and me we put a little report together," Liz explained. "We gave it to Alice's lawyers, complete with the pictures and the bank statements. You can just imagine the look on the ex-husband's face when he realised we were onto him. Turned out that the yacht had cost the best part of three hundred grand."

"Jesus!"

"And Elly would have had sod all if we hadn't helped her," Liz said. "That's what she said anyway when she gave us ten per cent. At first we didn't want to take it, but she insisted."

Bernie nodded. "You see, if she'd had to hire someone to do the same it would probably have cost her more. So there we were, thirty grand richer, and all of a sudden we had a business idea."

"The Wronged Women's Co-operative, although we take male clients on as well, of course. Kind of like a detective agency, but without the smoky offices and the sexy chicks in red velvet. We charge enough to make it a nice little side-line, although we don't get many thirty grand paydays. We don't ask for more money than anyone can afford. And we've actually got more work than we can handle! Once the word got out we've had people as far away as Edinburgh asking for our help. So now we're recruiting, looking for someone to take on a bit more of the admin side. Liz can do it, but she's busy with her day job. What do you think, Mary, you up for it?"

Bernie looked at her like it was already a done thing.

"Can I have a minute to talk to Liz? Alone?"

Mary tried hard to keep her face neutral as she followed Liz out to the living room. She waited until the door was closed, then gave the woman a venomous look.

"Is that why you recommended me for the job? Because of my… marital problems."

"Partly," Liz shrugged. She seemed surprised that Mary was annoyed. "Does it matter?"

"I am not a 'wronged woman', and I don't like people talking about my private life. It's not their business," Mary's cheeks were burning and she was struggling to keep her voice calm.

"That's not it at all. I actually thought you might be good at the job. And yes, I suppose I thought you would have some sympathy for our clients. But you needn't worry about the others. I haven't told them about your circumstances. Only that you could do with a bit of extra cash."

"Thank you." Mary took a deep breath. "I would rather keep it between us."

"There's no shame in being divorced, you know. It isn't the 1950s."

"I'm not divorced," Mary said sharply.

"Right. I forgot. Look, why don't we go back in? Bernie might let us have a scone."

Mary closed her eyes for a second. Think of the kids, she told herself, think of the cost of school uniforms. Think of not having to worry about money every bloody second of the day. She gave her shoulders a little shake, then stood up straight and followed Liz back into the dining room.

Chapter 14: Mary

"All right, now that that's all decided, let's get on with our current cases."

"Cases?" Liz frowned. "I thought we only had the one."

"I'll explain later. Mary, would you take notes?"

"Ah yes, of course." Mary pulled out her laptop and sat it on the table, glad that she had thought to bring it. She opened a new document and titled it Wronged Woman's Co-operative minutes: Meeting One.

"Right, well, we've been working on the case of Mrs Weston for the last few weeks. Liz, can you summarize for us?"

Liz put on a pair of serious black spectacles and pulled out a small tablet computer. Mary noted that it would have cost five times what she paid for her laptop.

"Our client is Mrs Vivienne Weston, Viv for short. Her uncle, Peter Weston, died at the grand old age of eighty-seven three months ago. Peter had married just two weeks before his death and left all his money to his new wife, despite earlier wills leaving the majority to our client. The new wife's name is Tiffany Baker – now Weston – and she is an alpaca farmer. She is also twenty-six years old. So far, so depressingly familiar. But here's the thing. Just before he died, Peter Weston told our client that he was regretting the marriage. That he had made a new will, removing the wife from his legacies, and hidden it somewhere. Our job is to try to find this new will."

Mary finished typing. "Wow," she said. "You really think there's a will hidden somewhere?"

Bernie shrugged. "That's what Viv Weston thinks. I'm not so sure. Viv cared for her uncle for years before he got married, and she was devastated when the young wife appeared on the scene. Could be that Peter was just trying to placate his niece by saying there was another will."

"On the other hand," Liz said, "we have the evidence of Peter's neighbours who heard several arguments between the married couple in the week before his death. Shouts in the middle of the night, that sort of thing."

"Was his death suspicious at all?"

Alice giggled. "You're wondering if the young wife bumped him off? No. He had a hernia op at the hospital and reacted to the anaesthetic. His heart was already a bit dodgy, and after three days in hospital it packed in."

Mary frowned, not quite ready to give up on the theory. "What about the arguments with his wife?"

"We asked her about them. Alice, tell her about the interview."

"Well, I told her I was writing a blog about alpacas. That got me in the door no problem, and when I asked about her dead husband, she didn't want to shut up! She was properly crying and everything. Said that they never argued. Her husband was totally supportive of her dreams. All alpaca-based, apparently. She wanted to expand the farm, make it into some sort of animal sanctuary or something. His legacy would let her do that. The only time she got bristly was when I mentioned the age gap. Love is love, she said, then she showed me the door. Honestly, I kind of liked her, even though she smelled of wet alpaca."

"It's not our place to like or not like the people involved," Bernie said sternly. "We have a job to do. This week's task is to search Peter Weston's house."

"Do you... um, need permission to do that?" Mary said tentatively, and she was sure she saw Liz roll her eyes.

"Viv still has a key so it's not breaking in. What do you reckon, Liz, you up for it?"

Liz shook her head. "Work is too crazy right now."

"I'll do it, Auntie," Alice said quickly. "Please!"

"No, it's too risky, how would you explain it if you were caught? I'll do it. I can go one evening. If anyone asks I'll say I'm collecting some equipment for the home or something. Much more plausible than if anyone else goes."

"That's settled then. Anything else?"

"Not on the Weston case, but I think there's something else we should look into."

"What's that?"

"The murder of Sam Jones."

Chapter 15: Mary

"Sam Jones? You don't mean, Mr Jones from the school?" Mary put her hand to her chest.

"That's the one," Bernie said, her cheeks flushed with excitement. "Turns out he wasn't hungover on Friday. He was dead."

"Christ," Liz said, putting down her glass. "Are you sure?"

"Happened on Thursday. They've not said officially, but my source is pretty sure. Did you know him well, Mary? Wasn't he your Vikki's teacher?"

"Not really. I mean, we've only been here for a few months. I met him once at the school for a settling-in day, and that was it." Mary tried to remember her impressions of the teacher. The kids had liked him, one of those younger teachers that tried to be cool, listening to music in class and letting them play computer games on a Friday. Mary hadn't approved of all that, although she hadn't said anything as she felt like it would have earned her an eye roll from the children. Mr Jones had been good looking, in a smooth way. The sort of guy that would spend a long time getting ready. Not her type. She liked men who thought moisturizer was the full extent of a beauty regime. She had never fancied going out with someone who had better eyebrows than she did.

"He's really dead then," Liz said. "Poor man, he could only have been in his thirties."

"Yes," Bernie continued. "That was what all the ambulances and police cars were for. They found his body in his car at the side of the road."

"How can you possibly know all this?" Mary asked.

"I have my sources."

Mary thought that Bernie might be enjoying her role as chief investigator a little too much.

"The question is," Liz said, tapping a long, painted nail against the table, "what do we do about it?"

There was a long pause.

"Well, nothing, I would have thought," Mary suggested. "I mean, from what you've told me you investigate marriage problems and missing teenagers. Isn't this a little out of your league?"

The silence developed a more pointed edge.

"I'm not saying you couldn't find out how he died," Mary added quickly. "I mean, you're obviously very good at what you do and everything. But isn't this kind of a step up from naughty ex-husbands?"

"She's got a point, Auntie," Alice said and Mary could have hugged the young woman for backing her up.

"She does not! You think the police will do better than us, do you? Find out who murdered the teacher when they don't know the first thing about this town and the people who live here. No, we are the best ones to investigate this."

Bernie was kind of scary, Mary thought. She was so fierce that it was hard to disagree with her. Maybe it hadn't been the best idea to take this job after all.

"We don't even know if he was murdered, do we?" Liz said. "I mean, if they found him dead in the car maybe it was just an accident. Some of these roads around here are dreadful if you drive a little too fast, and he seemed just the type to do that."

"Can't have been an accident. They've sent the Major Investigation Team down from Glasgow. Big Aggie who runs the Station Hotel told me a load of men in suits checked in this morning. By eleven o'clock they were moaning about the wifi and showed their badges to see if they could get special treatment."

"Huh. That does sound interesting," Liz said. "Maybe you're right Bernie, we could look into it."

"No one is paying you," Mary said, in a small voice. She was starting to realize that Bernie and Liz weren't interested in her opinion.

"True," Bernie shrugged. "But it'll keep our minds sharp. Think of it like a training exercise."

"Okay then," Alice said, "what do you want us to do?"

"Find out what Mr Jones was doing before he got killed," Bernie explained. "Ask around. We can start with the mums. And I guess the pubs. After all, we know he was a drinker."

"Hang on, who was it told you he was drunk on Friday?" Mary turned to Bernie. "In the playground, remember, you told me he was hungover."

66

"Wasn't it you?"

"No, I remember, it was you, Bernie, you told me. But then Liz came over and you'd heard that he was drunk as well."

"So I had," Liz nodded. "I think it was Frances Beatty who told me."

Bernie slapped her forehead. "Frances! That's right. She had cornered me at the school gates and ranted for ten minutes about Mr Jones and his 'inappropriate social life'." She gave the last three words air quotes.

"It seems to me, that maybe we should ask how Frances Beatty knew that Mr Jones was drinking the night he died," Mary said, her mind whirring.

Bernie laughed. "Aye, that's a good idea. Maybe Liz was right to take you on after all. Tomorrow morning you and I can go and see Frances and find out what she's playing at."

Mary's eyebrows shot up towards the ceiling. "Me? Aren't I just the secretary?"

"Don't do yourself down. Before long you'll be one of us."

"Oh good," Mary replied, and none of the others seemed to realise that she was being sarcastic.

Chapter 16: Mary

"What is this new job then?" Mary's mother, Nel asked. One of the reasons that Mary had moved to Invergryff was that her mother stayed in a small village just fifteen minutes away. Since the move, they had spent just about every Sunday there, in the comfortable home that smelled of freshly made bread and wildflowers. Nel herself was a domestic goddess, surrounded by homemade pickles and craft projects. Growing up, Mary hadn't appreciated just how much her mother had done around the house. Now that she was a mum herself she was beginning to think that Nel was some sort of witch.

"Oh, just a secretarial thing. But the hours are flexible so I can fit it around the kids."

"A bit strange that you're going out on a Sunday, isn't it?"

Mary looked down at her fingernails. "It won't be every week. They just want to fill me in on the systems they use, that sort of thing. Most of the time I'll be working from home."

"Well, I do think it's all a bit unnecessary. With the sort of wage Matt is on, surely you don't need to be taking a job at all."

Sometimes Mary wondered what century her mother was from.

"It's nice for me to have something outside of the kids."

"Well, of course it is. But wouldn't it make more sense to wait until Lauren is in school? They are only young once."

"It's not about the money," Mary lied.

"I know that, dear. But you will have to think about money at some point. I still don't understand why you're living in this tiny place when Matt still has the big house up north."

"It's only temporary," Mary said, "just until we manage to sell in Aberdeen and he comes down here to join us."

Nel looked like she was going to ask another question but Peter arrived from the back garden, blood dripping down his knee.

"Oh dear, were you climbing the tree again?" Nel reached for a cloth and applied a plaster. Mary was glad of the interruption. She had been lying about her life for so long now it had become second nature, but recently her mother had been asking more questions about Matt. At least the new job gave her something else to grill Mary on.

"And you're okay to have them here until after dinner," Mary asked, checking that she had everything she needed in her handbag.

"Of course. They're never any bother."

Annoyingly, that seemed to be true. The children that loved nothing more than drawing on the walls and flooding the bathroom floor in their own home seemed to become little angels when they were at their grandparents. Mary had often thought about installing some sort of spy camera to see exactly how they did it.

"All right, well, they've all got a change of clothes, just in case, and I've packed the tomato sauce that Johnny likes to eat on everything in the bag. I'll come and get them around half six if that's okay."

"Don't worry, dear, I've made shepherd's pie, they'll be fine."

"Only Lauren doesn't like meat at the moment and…"

"If their granny has cooked it, they'll eat it," Nel said firmly.

"Right." The worst thing was, they probably would, even though at home they wouldn't touch a bit of toast if it wasn't cooked entirely to their liking. Mary sighed. It would be nice to be away for a few hours.

Just a pity that she was going to spend it doing something that could get her arrested.

Chapter 17: Walker

So far, life attached to the Major Investigation Team was not turning out quite as DC Walker had hoped. He knew that he would be making the teas – that much was expected – but he had hoped he would at least get to attend some interviews, or do some door knocking. His first couple of days had been spent in front of a laptop, entering information that other people had collected into spreadsheets.

"Have you got the CCTV back from the pub?" Macleod asked. The Highlander was eating a bacon roll with one hand and typing into his computer with the other.

"The manager sent it over, but it was in a bad state," Walker explained. "The techs are cleaning it up now, hope to get it to us this afternoon."

"All right. The forensics have been no bloody help so far. Two sets of prints apart from the victim's in the car, but no matches. The CCTV better get us a look at this woman he was out with."

"Yes sir."

They had established fairly quickly where Sam Jones had spent his last twenty-four hours, thanks to his credit card transactions. The team had spoken to the barman who remembered Jones, but not much about his dining companion.

"A middle-aged woman," was all he could say, "probably blond. It was him I was looking at. He had a really nice

Omega, with a luminous dial. Must have cost him a good few thousand. Thought he might give a decent tip, but he only gave us a fiver."

Between the barman and a couple who had been sitting nearby, they had managed to get the vaguest of descriptions. A Caucasian woman in her thirties or forties, blond hair, medium build. Possibly wearing a big coat. Not exactly a photofit.

Walker's stomach rumbled. He looked at the Inspector's bacon roll with no little envy. He had a protein shake in his bag, but somehow it didn't quite appeal as much as the greasy smell coming from his colleague's breakfast.

There was a noise from the corridor and Detective Sergeant Neil Michelson burst into the room, looking excited. Walker knew him a little from the five-a-side football where he was fond of the sort of sliding tackle that made your fillings shake.

"Pathology results are back!"

Macleod jumped up, nearly knocking over a cup of tea. "Well, stick it up on the screen then."

A couple of clicks and the document appeared on the white smartboard. There were half a dozen people in the incident room and each of them moved forward to get a good view.

"Talk me through it," Macleod said.

"A couple of things came up in the post-mortem," the Sergeant said, pointing to the relevant sections. "I'll send out the summary later. There was frothy fluid on the lungs, which might suggest opioid misuse."

"Dilated pupils?" Macleod barked.

"Not detectable, unfortunately. Perhaps because it took so long to find the body. The toxicology reports are interesting. They found small amounts of morphine in his blood."

"Small amounts?"

"Doc says it's hard to detect definitively. This sample came from the bone marrow."

"Was there any sign he was a heroin user?"

Sergeant Mickelson shook his head. "No needle marks. Except for one." He clicked and the screen showed a close up of the victim's neck with a just discernible injection site. "The doctor went back and took another look at the body. This is the only needle mark on the body, and it's fresh."

"Then it's definitely murder."

"Looks like it. The pathologist is going to make a full report on Monday, but he's going to give opioid overdose as the cause of death. Hard to tell if it's heroin or something medical like diamorphine, apparently."

"Right." Macleod drummed his fingers on the table in front of him. "We will work on the likelihood that this injection was the cause of his death. We didn't find any defensive wounds on him so it was probably administered by someone he trusted. Where's my CCTV, constable?"

Chapter 18: Bernie

"How much trouble do you think we could get into for poking our noses into a murder investigation?" Mary asked.

Bernie ignored her. Honestly, she was already regretting agreeing to bring the woman onto the team. Liz had said she was bright and 'chronically underused' as a stay at home mum, but it turned out that Mary had a bad case of doing what she was told.

"Here's Frances's house," Bernie said, pointing at a smart new build with a large garden. "Now we just have to wait until quarter to twelve."

"What happens at quarter to twelve?"

"That's when Frances gets back from church. I told you she was old-fashioned, still drags the kids to Sunday school every week."

"Well, people should be free to practice their religion, shouldn't they?" Mary asked.

"Of course. I'm a good Catholic myself. Such a good Catholic that I haven't felt the need to step into a chapel for a decade."

"Huh," Mary said and looked out of the window. Bernie noted that she had a chocolate wrapper hanging out of her pocket. Perhaps she was in a sugar comedown. She'd give the woman some nutrition advice when she got a chance.

"There she is now." Bernie said, getting out of the car. It

wasn't hard to spot Frances's car. It was more bus than car, with enough seats for each of her five children.

"Hello," Bernie called out, giving the woman a wave.

"Hi Bernie," Frances called, helping a set of blond kids out of the car. "I wasn't expecting you?"

"No, sorry, I should have called. Only Mary and I were passing and I suddenly thought of some PTA business."

"Oh, that's quite all right," Frances's smile was wide with excitement. "PTA, you say? Joe, would you mind taking the kids in? We can sit in the garden if you like. I made fresh banana bread this morning if you'd like some."

"Yes please," Mary replied, coming forward. Bernie refrained from mentioning the amount of hidden sugar in homemade baked goods.

Frances's husband shepherded the children into the house. They were all dressed in identical smart shirts and shiny black shoes. Bernie was reminded of a movie where the kids all looked identical. What was it now? St Trinians? Just William? No, Children of the Corn, that was it.

Frances led the way around the house to the back garden with its perfectly manicured lawn and vegetable plots.

"Oh, how wonderful," Mary clapped her hands together. "Do you grow your own food?"

"When the Scottish weather allows," Frances replied, showing them towards a patio table and chairs. "Are you sure you'll be all right here, it's a little nippy. Only it'll be noisier inside."

"It's perfect," Bernie said, wrapping her coat more tightly against the wind. She didn't particularly want Frances's husband listening to their conversation. He was dull as ditch water and not much more intelligent. He played lawn bowls, which was enough to damn anyone in Bernie's book. Definitely not the right sort of person to be assisting in a gruesome murder.

"All right. I'll go get the banana bread. Teas all round?"

Bernie and Mary nodded and the woman disappeared into the house.

"So what's our strategy," Mary said, leaning towards Bernie and whispering like she was in some sort of dreadful TV drama.

"We just ask our questions and leave. It's not complicated."

"Can I be the good cop? I just know I'd be a terrible bad cop."

"Nobody is being any cop," Bernie tried not to let her irritation show. "We'll just try to find out what she knows about Mr Jones."

Mary looked a little disappointed, but at that moment the banana bread arrived and that seemed to cheer her up considerably.

"I don't know how you do it. Your house and garden are just lovely." Mary said, taking a large piece of banana bread and pulling it apart with her fingers.

"Thank you," Frances said, beaming once more.

Bernie glanced at Mary. She was quite extraordinarily pretty. The sort of face that would be described as elfin. And she seemed nice enough, if a little scatty. Wonder why the husband has buggered off, Bernie thought. According to Liz, she's two steps away from the breadline. And four kids as well. Shame. Anyway, time to get to the point.

"I suppose you've heard about Mr Jones."

Frances's lips curled downwards. "I couldn't believe it. They found him in his car, from what I heard. It's a nasty road that one."

"Mmn," Bernie sipped at her tea. "I was remembering that you told us he was hungover on the Friday morning. But of course, he wasn't."

"No," Frances said, a blush creeping over her cheeks. "I was wrong about that one."

"Why did you think it in the first place?" Mary asked.

"Well, now, I'm not sure I should say. Don't speak ill of the dead and all that."

Bernie decided to turn the screw a little. "But Frances, don't you think it might be PTA business, if there was something suspicious about his death?"

"Suspicious? What do you mean?"

Bernie didn't want to give too much away. "You see, we're worried it will reflect badly on the school if he was up to anything... unsavoury."

Frances's eyes nearly popped out of their sockets. "Oh dear, it couldn't be anything like that, could it? I mean, I didn't entirely approve of the man, dreadfully liberal, you see, but then again…"

"It would just be good to know, wouldn't it," Bernie pressed. "If we could find out what happened to him then we could be prepared for any fallout. Before it got into the *Gazette*."

"The *Gazette*? There wouldn't be anything in that dreadful rag would there?"

"Teacher drunk behind the wheel?" Mary did a mock shudder. "You can imagine the headline."

Frances put a hand to her chest. "Oh dear, do you think that was it? I mean, I know he was drinking, but surely not over the limit…"

"How do you know he was drinking?" Bernie pressed.

The woman sighed. "My sister saw him."

"Your sister? I didn't know you had a sister."

"Cheryl. I don't see her that much. She's ten years younger than me and to be honest, we don't have much in common. She doesn't have kids, doesn't have a boyfriend even. She's a bit 'alternative', if you know what I mean."

Bernie didn't, but it didn't seem the moment to ask.

"Anyway, Cheryl came around here on Friday morning before school. It was Rory's birthday, you see, and she wanted to drop off his present. She bought him some dreadful remote-controlled car with flashing lights, by the way. Of course, he loved it. We got to chatting and she said that she had seen Mr Jones in the pub on Thursday night and he was a bit the worse for wear for drink. So sad, really, when that happens."

"When what happens?"

"When a man can't control the drink. Thank goodness my husband doesn't take anything stronger than tea."

Might make him a bit more exciting if he did, Bernie thought. "Would you give us Cheryl's address?" she asked, standing up to go.

"Sure, I'll text you it. You haven't had your banana bread. Do you want me to wrap it up for you?"

"No thank you. I'm actually gluten intolerant."

"Oh dear," Frances said, as if it was somehow her fault. "I could bring you something else."

"Not at all. We should be going anyway."

Five minutes later they were back in the car. Bernie tried not to notice that Mary was shedding crumbs all over the passenger seat.

"I didn't realise you were gluten intolerant," Mary said while Bernie put Cheryl's address into her satnav. "That must make things difficult."

"Oh, I'm not allergic."

"Really?"

"I just don't eat cake. Look, I brought something else with me to snack on."

Bernie brought out the plastic container from her bag.

"What are those?" Mary asked.

"Protein bites. Made with nut butter and chai seeds. Want one?"

"No thanks."

Bernie shrugged. Some people were beyond her help.

Chapter 19: Walker

It took a further two hours before the CCTV came through and by this point, Macleod was climbing the walls. When the technician arrived with the file on a memory stick, the Inspector snatched it from her hand and put it up on the screen.

"Talk me through it."

The young technician swallowed, then stood up next to the screen. Jenny was her name, Walker remembered, a woman in her early twenties with hair tightly pinned back in a bun and a permanently nervous expression.

"Okay, so we had to do some sharpening up. The CCTV system is pretty old, as you can tell, and the frame speed isn't great. We've put it through our imaging software and here are some of the clearest shots of your victim and the suspect."

The first image showed Sam Jones from behind, walking into the pub. He had a smart jacket on and his hand was pressed against his companion's back.

Macleod squinted at the screen. "We can see a little of her outfit here. Long skirt and what do you think – sandals?"

Jenny nodded. "We think so. And I'm not sure about the skirt. She's got a long coat on so it might be covering the length. Light-coloured, Macintosh style."

"Right. Next picture."

"This is them on their way back out of the pub. He's walking slightly ahead of her, so he's between her and the camera, but we should be able to see her face. Only we can't.

The woman was walking strangely, with one arm upstretched so that the coat was covering half her face.

Macleod's bushy eyebrows lowered into a frown. "It looks like she's shielding her face."

"We think she's aware of the cameras," the technician said. "Every time she's in the car park she had her hand to her face."

"And what can we get from that?"

Walker sat up straight in his seat. "Premeditation, Sir. She was planning to kill him. Otherwise, why would she hide her face?"

"Could be, but I can think of a few other reasons. An affair perhaps? It's not concrete evidence of premeditation so far." Macleod clicked back through the images, staring at the woman as if he could summon her with his eyes. "But on balance I suspect you're right, Walker. She doesn't want her face shown because she does not want to be identified. And that makes her our number one suspect."

"I'll pick out the best images," Jenny said, turning off the screen. "You're not going to have anything that will give you a definitive identification."

"Send me what you can and we'll get it out to the press. We've kept this quiet so far but hopefully a member of the public will be able to identify her. You never know."

Macleod's morose expression suggested he wasn't holding out hope.

"Right, let's take these images and get on the streets. Neil, are the parents still staying locally?"

Sergeant Mickelson nodded. "Yes sir. They're at the hotel with the liaison officer."

"Go round and talk to them, see if they recognise the woman from the CCTV."

Mickelson gathered up his things and left the room.

"All right, Constable Walker, I want you to come with me to the school. Let's see if anyone there recognises this woman. Then we'll go and take another look around the victim's house and see if we can find any hint of her there. So far she is our only suspect, and we know next to nothing about her."

Walker grabbed his coat and hurried out after the Inspector. This was more like it! A chance to see how the MIT worked out in the field.

"Is there a decent coffee shop around here?" Macleod asked.

"Yes, just on the high street. It's an Italian place, Russo's."

"Great. I knew your local knowledge would come in handy."

Walker tried not to be offended. He had been hoping that the Inspector had chosen him over his razor-sharp investigative skills, not his ability to find a good coffee shop.

When they got to Russo's it was Walker that got out and ordered the Inspector his flat white while the older man stayed in the car answering emails.

"Let's go to Jones's house first," Macleod said, not looking up from his tablet, "then we can try and catch the school at lunchtime."

"It's Sunday, sir," Walker reminded him.

"Damn! Send a message to base and ask if they can find the head teacher's home address, we'll try there instead. Jones's house first."

Walker complied but just as they pulled up outside the victim's home, Macleod's phone rang.

"Hope you don't mind if I take a personal call?"

"Not at all."

Macleod picked up his mobile and spoke into it quietly. Walker got out of the car to give him some privacy. Sam Jones had lived in a small semi-detached seventies house, identical to every other on the estate. Recently recovered in stark white render, this sort of house had always made Walker think of rows of teeth, all packed in together. He much preferred his flat in an old tenement, a bit of character, even if it did cost a fortune to heat.

The front garden of Jones's house was laid to gravel, with a sad little rose bush stuck in a pot at the front door. Not much of a gardener, by the looks of things.

Macleod turned off the phone and walked back to the door.

"Everything okay, Sir?"

"My wife. Her mother's not been well and it makes her a little… Well, anxious I suppose. I tried to tell her we're hardly likely to be done in by the Krays in deepest darkest Renfrewshire, but she worries. She likes to know where I am. You would think that being married to a copper for a decade would have stopped that somehow. You married, son?"

"No sir."

"Well, you should get married."

Walker laughed. "I'm not sure it's quite that simple."

"Sure it is. Your snowflake generation, you think that everyone has to be perfect. I bet that if you walked into any bar you would find half a dozen women that would make you a lovely wife. Or are you gay? I'm sure you'd find just as many handsome men, if that's your thing."

This time he raised an eyebrow at the Inspector. "Not gay. Just not interested in marriage."

"Your supper cooked for you when you get home? A little bit of warmth on a cold winter's evening? What's not to like?"

Walker couldn't help but chuckle. "I'm not sure all women like to make a man's supper for when they get home anymore, sir."

"That's not what I meant. I do as much housework as the missus does. More even, given that she doesn't know how to stack the dishwasher. You think I'm ancient, don't you? Look, I'm not fifty yet, but I've learned a few things about relationships over the years. Most people just need someone to be nice to them, someone they can be nice to as well. Simple as that."

85

"Well, I'll do my best, sir."

"See that you do. Best thing for a copper is a happy home life. Stops them from getting down when they have a bad day on the job. I don't like it when my lads go home, drink by themselves and then each morning becomes harder to get up for. You'll be Sergeant by the end of the year, and looking at CID maybe after that if you do well on this case. Just don't let it get on top of you."

"I won't, sir," Walker said, then he walked towards the house, eager to escape the conversation. "Shall we go inside?"

Chapter 20: Mary

"I thought we were going to Cheryl's house," Mary said, picking a crumb of banana cake from the cuff of her coat. "Didn't Frances say it was over on the other side of town?"

"Just a quick stop first."

Mary checked that her seatbelt was still fastened. Bernie had the driving style of someone who knew the local roads a little too well. She took every corner at the highest speed possible without actually causing an accident. The driving, combined with the banana cake was giving Mary the most peculiar feeling in her stomach.

"Here we are." Bernie bounced out of the car and was halfway up the drive before she had a chance to ask where they were.

It wasn't unlike Frances Beatty's house, except far smaller. Built around the seventies with the white render and anthracite grey windows that seemed to be the fashion at the moment. Soulless. Mind you, Mary thought ruefully, it probably doesn't have mushrooms growing in the bathroom.

"Where are we…" Mary trailed off as she watched Bernie bypass the front door and head for the gate to the back garden. "Oh god."

She caught up with the nurse and grabbed her arm. "This isn't Mr Jones's house, is it? Please tell me it isn't."

"I don't like lying," Bernie said as she slipped her hand

through the gate to open the latch. "Got it! One of my sisters stays in this estate, just a couple of streets away. They've all got these latches you can open from the outside. Terrible security."

"We can't go in there!"

"Listen, we're not going to break in or anything. I just thought we could have a look around, get a feel for the place, maybe have a peek in the windows. He died in his car, not at the house, remember?"

Mary chewed at her knuckles in indecision. Damnit, she was already standing at the gate, at least in the garden she wouldn't be visible to anyone walking past. She followed Bernie inside and pulled the gate shut behind her.

Bernie hurried over to the patio door, cupping her hands around her face so that she could see in.

"Huh. He's got dirty dishes in the sink. Not much else to see though. Horrible glass table, always makes you think that you're going to smash it when you put a cup down."

Mary looked up at the house, and nearly fell backwards when she noticed a curtain twitch.

"Jesus! There's someone in there!"

Bernie was over in a flash. "Is there? Hang on, that's next door, not Mr Jones's place."

"It means they saw us walking around the garden though," Mary said. She was feeling thoroughly unsettled, even though the person in the window had disappeared.

"Geoff something," Bernie said, picking up flower pots and looking underneath them. "He used to have a wife at the home. A crabbit old thing he is, pretty much housebound. You don't need to worry about him."

In spite of Bernie's not-entirely-reassuring words, Mary wandered as far away from the house as she could. She didn't even want to look through the windows. Despite Bernie's assurances, she wasn't sure that it wouldn't be some sort of crime.

The end of the garden looked onto a patch of waste ground and brambles were growing through the hedge. She picked a ripe blackberry and popped it into her mouth.

"Grass needs cut," Bernie said.

"Maybe he was into the rewilding thing. You know, letting things grow naturally."

"Lazy, more like. Why don't you check out that shed?"

Mary walked over to the six foot square wooden shed and peered in through the window. There was a bike there, possibly an expensive one. Matt had had something similar. Bought as an economical alternative to owning a second car, it had somehow ended up costing more than anything with an engine ever would have done. Every week some new item of bike equipment arrived, to be rushed away to the shed.

Was Mr Jones a bike fiend like Matt? Mary made a note to ask Bernie if he cycled to school. It hardly seemed relevant, but this was her first time trying to be a detective, and she was determined not to miss anything.

Not that she was planning on doing too much 'detecting', Mary reminded herself. She was a secretary, that's all, even if the idea of being a modern-day Miss Marple was quite appealing. She took another look into the shed to see if there was anything she'd missed. There was a poster on the wall, an old map of the world like you would see in student digs. Some garden tools that looked as shiny as when they were new. She shuffled closer, trying to avoid the cobwebs when a bang at the gate made her stand up straight.

Unfortunately, she had forgotten about the eaves of the shed and cracked her head right on the top.

"Ouch!"

"Are you all right?" A strange voice called out from the garden gate.

Mary rubbed at her head. She would probably have a lump there later.

"Let me see."

Her eyes were watering, but she could see someone tall coming over. Tall and… yes… very good looking with a strong jaw and just a hint of stubble. A handsome man with something in his hand.

"Any blood?"

"No, I think I'm okay. Um."

Oh god. A tall handsome man holding out a police ID card.

"My name is Constable Walker. Can I ask if you have

permission to be in this garden?"

Bernie walked towards them. "We're friends of one of the neighbours. They wanted someone to check that poor Mr Jones's house hadn't been left unlocked."

Constable Walker's expression didn't change. "Which neighbour was that?"

Even though Mary's heart was in overdrive with stress, it was quite nice to see Bernie discomfited.

"Well, they are called..."

She's going to tell him more lies, Mary realised with growing horror. She needed to step in.

"Sorry, officer. We actually just let ourselves in. Our kids were in Mr Jones's class and when we heard he'd died... Well, we wanted to find out what happened."

Bernie clearly wasn't happy with this. "We wanted to find out what the police weren't telling us. You know, about his murder."

The Constable twitched his lower lip. Mary couldn't tell if he was amused or annoyed.

"This is a police investigation. Members of the public will find out when an arrest is made."

"And when will that be?" Bernie said, jutting out her chin. "Someone needs to tell the local people what's happening. And that's us."

"So you're what..."

"We're journalists."

Mary tried not to react to yet another audacious lie.

"For which paper."

"It's a website, actually," Bernie continued. "A community action group. Parents, mainly. We're concerned that there might be a threat to our children."

"And what makes you think that?"

"Well, it was a teacher that was killed, wasn't it?"

Walker was starting to look a little weary. There was something about talking to Bernie that ground you down. She never gave an inch.

"We only walked around the garden," Mary said, using her most apologetic tone. "We'll leave right now."

"And you won't come back?"

"Of course not," she said. Bernie said nothing.

"Give me your names then and you can go on your way."

They did as the police officer asked, then hurried out of the garden and back to the car.

Mary's heart was pounding, but she couldn't help smiling a little.

"It was a bit exciting, wasn't it?" She said to Bernie as the engine started up.

"Huh. We might have got somewhere if that policeman hadn't

shown up."

"What could we tell from the outside of someone's house?"

"Well, nothing." Bernie smirked and took something out of her pocket. "But I'd only just found the spare keys."

Mary took in a sharp breath. "Bernie! You need to tell the police! I can't believe you took them."

"Officer pretty face and his pals will have Mr Jones's keys, won't they? We'll keep these, just in case."

Mary bit her lip. There was no point in arguing with the woman. Even the police weren't a match for Bernie Paterson and her unbending belief that she was always doing the right thing.

Chapter 21: Walker

Constable Walker watched the two women leave. The thin, fierce one held her head high all the way back to the car, while the quiet one scurried after her. He checked his notes. Mary Plunkett, that was the latter's name. Very attractive, which was always a bit unfortunate when it was someone he met on the job. Not that she was involved in the case, so there would be nothing to stop him… Well, best not to. After all, they were clearly both more than a little unhinged.

"Nothing worse than bored housewives and curtain twitchers," Macleod said as the car drove away. "I hope you sent them on their way."

"They said they were from the press."

"Bollocks. Do they look like press to you?"

"No. One of them had a uniform on. A nurse or a carer I think."

"Did you get their names?"

He nodded.

"Well, as long as they're not fake names then we can always chase them up, but in my experience towns like this are always full of local busybodies. Often think they know the job better than we do. You can imagine what it's like when I go back up to Shetland. The ultimate small town mentality. Can't pump up your tyres without someone coming over and telling you how their taxpayers' money could be better spent than on lazy old policemen."

Macleod drifted off into angry silence, the keys jangling in his closed fist.

"Um, sir? Are we going to go inside?"

The Inspector looked up. "Yes, we are. Now, I want you to keep an open mind when we go in here. Forensics have already been, so we don't need to watch where we step, although we'll go in gloves and overshoes just in case. What we're looking for here is anything that'll give us clues to his private life, anything that might look out of place. And I'd like to find any evidence of the woman from the pub."

"What about his phone?"

"Access should come through on Monday. Apparently, Silicon Valley doesn't work weekends. Until we get the passwords we'll rely on old school policing. Without the beating up of suspects, of course."

"Of course."

"That was a joke, Constable. You could try cracking a smile."

The Inspector unlocked the front door and they walked into the hall. It was a narrow building, with a living room at the front and a kitchen behind. Walker thought that when it had been built it would have been seventies chic with swirly carpets and Artex ceilings. Sam Jones, in contrast, had painted every wall white, with grey carpets and modern, flat-pack furniture. The living room was just as bland as the grey hallway. A makeshift desk had been set up in one corner, and there was an

L-shaped sofa with a large flat-screen television on the wall opposite. No pictures hung on the walls and apart from a sideboard from ikea, there was no other furniture.

"Definitely a bachelor pad," Macleod said, standing in the middle of the room. "Not enough cushions for there to be a girlfriend."

"Isn't that a bit sexist?"

"Might be. But it's true that cushions multiply around women. I can barely sit down on my own sofa without sinking into a dozen of the damned things."

"Right." Walker noticed a small bookshelf with a collection of paperback thrillers on the top shelves and some file folders on the bottom. "Will I go through these?"

"Sure. I'll take the desk."

Walker took his time to examine every item on the bookcase. He removed all the books and flicked through them, checking the shelves behind to see if anything was hidden. Then he started to open the folders, but was quickly disappointed.

"It's all schoolwork. Lesson plans, that sort of thing."

"Go through it quickly then," Macleod said, "we don't need to know how he was teaching the kids their ABCs."

"Unless that's why he was murdered."

"What, you think some parent got upset because their precious little one got a telling off? No, I don't buy it. It's not like they use the cane these days. Unless… no hints that he had an unhealthy interest in the kids?"

Walker paused. "Not that I've heard." He really hoped it wasn't going to be that sort of case.

"We'll find out when we get the password for his laptop. Until then, open mind."

It took them two hours to make their way through the desk and shelves, but there was little of note.

"I've got a letter here to a Mr Victor Smelter, but at this address," Macleod said, holding up a letter.

"Previous owner, maybe?"

"Could be." Macleod ripped the paper open. "Just spam mail for a holiday company. Well, if that's the best we've got we'd better hope there's something upstairs."

There were only two bedrooms, Jones's room and a second that seemed to be used mainly for storage and a pull-out bed. Again, the décor was bland and lacking in personality. It was as if the man was determined to spite their attempts to find out anything about him.

The master bedroom was smart, impersonal and had some expensive bedding.

"Linen, from John Lewis," Macleod said. "The wife likes them," he added after catching Walker's curious expression.

The Constable moved onto the mirrored wardrobes which were full of clothes. Around half looked like shirts for work, but the other half were designer brands, many of them in silky materials.

"He liked a smart shirt," Walker said. "And these jeans are expensive, sir."

"Not short of money, then. What did his bank records say?"

"HQ is still working through them, but there was no debt and a fair amount saved up. Nothing out of the ordinary for a teacher's salary."

"Where did he spend his money? Online or in the town. Glasgow maybe? That should give us some idea of what he was getting up to."

"Not sure, sir. I can check when we get back."

"Hmmn," Macleod said and turned back to the search. Walker was annoyed with himself, he should have checked the bank statements earlier. He needed to prove that he could show initiative if he wanted to impress his boss.

There was a chest of drawers next to the bed and Walker opened and shut each one in turn. Jones was fairly organised, with each item of clothing in a particular place. The bottom drawer was full of t-shirts, and he was about to shut it when he saw a flash of colour underneath.

"Some lads' mags in this drawer, sir."

Macleod chuckled and came around to have a look. "Thought it was all online these days. Well, his taste looks to be people of legal age at least. Woman, rather than men too, which makes it more likely he was on a date at the pub. I wish we could identify the bloody woman. It's not like this is a big town. Someone must know her. Any news from the other officers?"

The Constable checked his messages. "Not so far. Jenny has sent the images out and they'll be in the national papers and social media tomorrow."

"The local busybodies will love that. Well, hopefully we'll get a name. Until we do we need to keep our options open. We need to find some other people of interest. Ideally before I meet with the Super on Monday afternoon."

Walker closed the final drawer. "That's it, sir, all clean."

The Inspector stood up from his examination under the bed and winced when his knees made a cracking sound. "We better hope that there's something on his phone or laptop. Otherwise, we've got nothing. The man was a ghost even before someone killed him."

Chapter 22: Bernie

"I can't be late picking the kids up," Mary said for the third time.

Bernie pushed through the amber traffic light, ignoring the idiot honking his horn behind her. "Don't worry, we've only got to stop in at Cheryl's house and then we'll head back."

"Then you'll call the police about the keys."

"Sure," Bernie replied, meaning no such thing. She wished Liz was with her. The new girl was a definite wet blanket. One day she must find out how mousy little Mary Plunkett had gotten the courage to leave her husband, but not today. Today they had work to do.

"I think this is the street," Mary said, peering at the sign. "Yes, that's it, block C."

Cheryl's flat was a contrast from her sister's place. It was part of a 1960's tower block that was around ten stories high. It had recently been spruced up, given a coat of stark white render, but it only made it look more alien compared to all the Victorian terraces around it.

"Looks like one sister got all the money," Bernie said walking past the lift for the metal stairwell. "Come on, it's a chance to work those thigh muscles."

Mary let out a tiny groan behind her, but Bernie pretended not to notice. The woman's cardiovascular system could definitely do with a workout. Besides, she needed to get her own steps in. She normally did fifteen thousand a day, but she'd spent too long in the car. By the time they reached Cheryl's flat on the sixth floor, she was beginning to feel calmer.

"Jesus wept," Mary said, leaning against the wall. "That was a lot of stairs." Her face had gone an unattractive mauve colour.

Bernie rolled her eyes and then rang the doorbell.

"Hello?" A slim woman with dark hair and a nose stud opened the door.

"We're friends of your sister's," Bernie said. "We were wondering if we could pop in for a chat."

"Okay," Cheryl shrugged and walked away, leaving them to show themselves in.

Inside, the flat was rather smart. There was the sort of sixties-style furniture that Bernie could remember her parents throwing out when it got tatty, but now these hipster types seemed to have decided it was fashionable again. It did look good in this flat which, despite the low ceilings, was full of light from the large windows on one side.

Cheryl had curled up on an armchair, legs under herself like a small child. Bernie and Mary took the uncomfortable chesterfield sofa opposite.

"You'll have to be quick," Cheryl said. "And I've no milk so I can't offer you a cuppa."

"Don't worry about it," Mary said, giving the woman her best friendly smile. Bernie was quite happy for the woman to play good cop. No one would mind Mary Plunkett asking her questions, she was just too nice. "Thanks for letting us in."

"Frances called to let me know you were coming. I wish she would learn to keep her big mouth shut."

"You didn't want us to come and talk to you, then?" Bernie asked.

"There's nothing to tell. Yes, I saw Sam Jones in the pub. No, I didn't see who he was with. He was at the bar, paying the bill and I stayed out of his way. So there's nothing I can tell you or the police that would help."

Bernie's shoulders slumped. "Ah, that's a shame."

Meanwhile, Mary had got up from the sofa to look out of the window. The woman had the attention span of a gnat.

"What a view there is out here!"

"It's great isn't it?" Cheryl flashed a brief smile. "You can see Glasgow on a clear day."

"It's amazing. Come look, Bernie, I can see my house from here!"

"No thank you."

"Oh come on, I can see the church on the corner! You know, the one that's the Rennie Macintosh knock-off."

"I don't like heights, okay?"

Mary looked shocked. "Really? I didn't think you were afraid of anything."

"It's a natural evolutionary instinct," Bernie said firmly, getting off the sofa while making sure she kept her back to the window. "Well, if you've nothing to tell us, I suppose we should be going."

"I just wondered," Mary said softly, "how did you know it was Sam Jones you saw in the pub?"

"Oh, I went on a date with him once, didn't Frances tell you? Why do you think I left the pub so quickly? It would have been kind of awkward if he had recognised me."

"You dated Mr Jones?" Bernie asked. She wondered why Frances had omitted that piece of information.

Cheryl laughed. "You make it sound like we were engaged or something. We went on one date. That's all. He most definitely was not my type, and that was that."

Bernie lowered herself back onto the sofa.

"It would be great if you could tell us about the date," Mary said. "Just so we can get a better impression of what sort of guy he was."

"Why's it matter to you anyway?" Cheryl asked.

"Well, we're trying to stop his death from becoming a big scandal. Your sister is worried that the school will end up in the paper."

"Of course she is. Heaven forbid anything might happen that the Church would disapprove of. I don't give a rat's ass what my sister thinks, if you want the truth."

Mary leaned forward. "To be honest with you, we don't care either. We're just trying to find out who killed him. After all, it's a small town and none of us like the idea of some murderer being on the loose."

"He was murdered, then?"

"Looks like it."

Cheryl rubbed her chin. "Funny that. I wouldn't have thought he was interesting enough for someone to murder him. I don't even know why I went out with him. I'd just broken up with a guy I'd been seeing for over a year. And I guess I was just a bit vulnerable or something. He came over to me in Glasgow when I was having lunch in a coffee shop, and he was good looking, a bit like a footballer or something. Looked after himself, you know? He asked if I wanted to go out for dinner, and I thought it might be nice."

"Was it not nice?"

"It was pretty dire. We had absolutely nothing in common. It was clear from about five minutes in that he only asked me because he thought I'd be an easy shag. Despite what my sister might have told you, one-night stands aren't my thing. Especially with someone who spoke like my dad."

"Did he seem like he was worried about anything?" Bernie asked.

Cheryl shrugged. "Not that I could tell. This was three months ago, so I guess if someone was going to crash into him, he'd hardly have been worried about it, would he?"

Interesting, Bernie thought, that she thinks it was a car crash.

According to what she'd heard from Mrs Battaglia, the car hadn't been touched.

"We just don't know yet," Mary said, continuing her questioning. "But anything you can tell us might help. Was there anything strange about the date at all?"

"There was one funny thing. When I said I lived in town, he said he didn't normally date people from here. Well, I was all ready to be offended by that, but he said that it was because he didn't want to accidentally date one of the mums from school, which I guess is fair enough."

"Anything else?" Bernie asked.

Cheryl flicked a strand of hair from her face. "I got the feeling he did it a lot."

"What, drank?"

"No, dated. He had all these cheesy lines ready to go, like he'd said them a thousand times. He was smooth, you know?"

"And you didn't see him again?"

"Not until Thursday night. He was over the other side of the bar, paying the bill. He looked a bit worse for wear, not falling over drunk, but pretty tipsy. I walked away from him before he could recognise me and that was it."

"And you never saw the woman?"

"No. But I bet there was one. He was the sort of person who if he wasn't with a woman, he was already looking around for the next date. When we went out I'm pretty sure he asked the waitress for her number."

"Sounds like an awesome guy. Thanks for speaking to us, and I do think you should call the police," Mary said, "just to tell them what you told us."

"Okay," Cheryl said, "if you think it's worth it."

Bernie checked her watch. "We'd better go."

"Yes," Mary stood up too. "Thank you for all your help."

"It's fine," Cheryl said and let them show themselves out.

Bernie drove Mary home. She made sure to drive quickly so that Mary could get to her parents' house on time, but the woman didn't look too grateful. She pulled up on the double yellow line outside and put her hazards on.

"I'll see you tomorrow night for an emergency WWC meeting," Bernie said. "I'll send one of the N's round to watch the kids."

"Thanks. Wow, I didn't think knuckles really went white."

"What?"

"Nothing. Thanks for the lift. It's been an interesting day."

"No problem. What are your bank details?"

"Sorry?"

"Your bank details. I'll transfer your pay for today. You've done, what, five hours in the car with me today? We'll round it up to six. I'll send you the hundred and eighty over right away."

"Thirty pounds an hour? Isn't that a bit much for a secretary?"

"You asked some good questions in there. Maybe you'll be more than the admin girl before long."

"Do you think so?"

"Sure," Bernie said. "If you can loosen up a bit. Off you get and see those kids of yours. I'll see you in the playground tomorrow."

Chapter 23: Liz

The worst thing about Monday morning, Liz thought, was that the dread of it started on Sunday night. She had lain awake until long after Dave was snoring in bed next to her, thinking about having to go into the office. Often the reality wasn't as bad as she imagined. Sometimes it was even worse.

Her firm had a main office in Glasgow with a hundred people working there, but in Invergryff there were only a dozen of them. It might have been easier if there were more people there, Liz thought, slipping into her office. Easier to go unnoticed in a crowd.

At least she had arrived early. Her mum had agreed to take Sean to school so that she could get to work first thing. Dave could have done the school run, but he'd been feeling a little 'rough' after the conference. Picked up a cold from somewhere, he said, although Liz thought it was probably just a hangover. Still, he hardly ever went out these days so she didn't begrudge him it.

Liz sipped at her takeaway coffee. Easier, of course, to go to the communal kitchen and make one, cheaper too, but there was always the risk of who she might bump into.

"Hi, Liz," a perky voice called. "Have you got a minute?"

"Of course."

Amy walked in and flashed her a smile. Liz still found the trend for overly contoured makeup and false eyelashes in young women startling. It was like working with a beautiful cyborg.

"Did you have a good weekend?"

"Quiet," Liz said. "You?"

"Nothing much. There was this pop-up music festival so I went to some of that during the day. Oh, and I was out on Saturday night and I think I'm still hungover. Didn't get home until five."

"Five AM? God, I'm glad I'm an old woman now. No way could I stay up that late."

"You're not old," Amy replied, with the tone of someone who thought Liz was about ready for a cemetery plot. "Anyway, I wondered if you could take a look at the latest Davidson file for me. There's something weird going on with the expenses column and I think I must have made a mistake somewhere."

"Of course. Ping it over to me."

"Will do. Oh, and Phil wants to see you. He got in at six this morning. I swear, the guy has no social life whatsoever."

Liz ducked her head so that Amy couldn't see her expression. "No problem. I'll go right up."

Get it over with, Liz thought, and she stood up, leaving the second half of her coffee to go cold in the cup. She walked across the office and up a single flight of stairs to where the managers were.

She knocked on the office of Managing Director Philip

Hornby.

"Come in."

Younger than her, white with dark hair that was starting to recede a little around the temples, Phil displayed a bright white smile. He clicked off his laptop, not before she could see the website for a posh estate agency up in the background.

"Liz. Long time no see."

"We spoke on Thursday," Liz replied. She went over to the chair on the other side of the desk and pulled it out so that she was sitting as far as possible away from him.

"Is that so? I've been trying to get hold of you for several days now."

"I'm aware of that. It was the weekend."

Liz adjusted her polo neck. When she had started at the firm she used to wear whatever she liked, as long as it was smart. Now she would never think of wearing anything that suggested she was trying to look too available.

"Listen, Phil, I don't want any trouble here."

"Trouble?" Phil smiled again. It reminded her of the way that snakes liked to open their jaws before swallowing their prey. "Why would there be any trouble?"

Liz leaned forward. "Messaging me at the weekend is not appropriate at all, Phil. You know that. It's harassment."

"That's a nasty word to use, Liz. Of course, we know who's harassing who, don't we?"

Liz pinched the bridge of her nose. "Why don't you just tell me why you asked me in here? There better have been a reason."

"Of course. You don't think I just wanted to see your pretty face, do you?" There were tiny flecks of saliva on his lips. "I need the latest timelines for the West beach project. It needs to have full calculations on man hours."

"That's not due until the end of the month."

"I know. But Ollie asked me for them today and I said you would get right on it. Liz Okoro is reliable, I said, she'll get it done by end of play tomorrow."

"But you know that I've already got the monthly documents to file. And the patents. I don't have time to look at it."

Phil leaned back in his chair until the front legs came off the floor. Liz prayed hard to any deity going that he would fall onto his face.

"I'm doing you a favour here. If you pull this off then Ollie will think you're a shoe-in for your next promotion. We both know how important that is to you."

Liz curled her lip, about to say something, then she swallowed. "Look Phil, I don't want to create a problem here."

"Sure you don't. That's why you're going to get those files for me. Tomorrow."

"This is some stupid power play, isn't it?" Liz said, unable to contain herself.

"Not at all. I'd ask the same of anyone here. No one else has a problem with being a team player, apart from you."

"Do you really think that you're treating me fairly?"

"Fair? You think I'm being unfair?"

"I think that you are being unduly influenced by what happened last Christmas."

There was a beat of silence.

"Didn't we agree not to bring that up?" Phil said, the grin absent for the first time. "That it would do too much damage to both of us if it ever got out?"

"Yes, we did," Liz said, trying not to grind her teeth.

"Well then, if we're both on the same page, you better get back to work. You've got a lot of hours to put in before five o'clock on Tuesday."

Screw you, Phil, Liz screamed inside her head. Instead, she got up and left his office, managing somehow not to slam the door on the way out.

There was a buzz as her phone got a text. For a wild moment, she thought Phil had sent it, just to wind her up even more, but it was Bernie.

Police have confirmed murder. Check Gazette webpage for news. See you tonight for the meeting. Bernie.

Why was it, Liz thought, that people like Philip Hornby never got murdered and innocent school teachers did instead? There was no justice in the world, she thought as she tried to work out how to tell Bernie she wouldn't make the meeting. It was time to think of another lie.

Chapter 24: Liz

As if she didn't have enough on her mind, Liz got a call from her husband just half an hour after her meeting with Phil.

"The school called. We forgot to give Sean his gym kit this morning."

"No, we didn't," Liz said, one hand still typing out an email to a contractor. "I picked it up and put it in the car, right next to my handbag." She looked down at her handbag, a rather nice Mulberry one in tan leather. And the plastic tote bag next to it.

"Damn!"

"You forgot then?"

"Looks like it. I'll run it in for him."

"Great. How's work?" Dave asked.

Awful, Liz wanted to say, but didn't. "Fine. Busy as usual. I'll take an early lunch and drop the bag off now."

"Have a good one. See you later," Dave clicked off the call.

The drive back to the school went by in a flash. Liz's mind was on the project, and how she could get it done before the deadline. She refused to give Phil the satisfaction of seeing her fail. When she pulled up at the school she got out of the car, only to realise she had left the bag inside again. She pulled it off the seat and took a few deep breaths.

This can't go on, Liz thought. If she didn't manage to stop Phil from getting into her head like this, it wouldn't just be gym bags she would start losing. She had to do something drastic, and soon.

"Can I help you?" A voice said from the playground. There was a young woman hurrying over to her, her arms full of photocopying.

"Yes, I…" Just as Liz began to speak a sudden gust of wind pulled the paper from the girl's hands, scattering them around her like confetti.

"Oh no!" The girl's mouth turned down as she realised there was no chance of catching them while her arms were still full of the rest of the papers.

"Don't worry, I'll get them."

A few minutes of frantic grabbing and some rather unattractive jogging around the playground and Liz had managed to collect all the paper and replace it on the pile, albeit rather more crumpled than before.

"Sorry, I'm just so clumsy." The girl said. Liz might have mistaken her for a high school pupil if it wasn't for the lanyard hanging around her neck. "I'm Niamh, I work at the school."

"No problem," Liz said, trying not to show how hard she was panting. She really needed to find time to get to the gym.

"Thank you so much!" Niamh said. She had the sort of pale Scottish skin that looks almost blue, with blond hair pulled back into a tight bun. She looked like she was half ghost, not entirely there. "Are you going into the school?"

"Oh no, I just wanted to drop off this gym kit for my son. Sean, he's in primary five."

The woman smiled. "I can take that for you if you like."

"Thank you." Liz said. She noticed that the woman had red-rimmed eyes, like she had been crying recently. "I guess everyone is a bit preoccupied at the moment. What with the death of poor Mr Jones and all."

The girl flinched like someone had hit her. "God, it's just been so, so awful. I mean, I never thought that anything like this would happen."

Her huge blue eyes become like watery puddles.

"No, I suppose you wouldn't," Liz replied. "Did you know him well?"

"Oh, not that well," Niamh said. "I'm a teaching assistant, so I helped out in his class sometimes, but that was all. I never went out with him."

I never thought you did, Liz almost said, but decided that would be a little too cruel. Even Sam Jones with his reputation for the ladies would have more sense than to date this young colleague. It was weird to think of her even dating, like Casper on tinder or something. Unless…

Liz's phone buzzed. On reflex, she took it out and looked at the message. *Boss wants to see you about irregularities in the Bloom file.*

She didn't need to check the number to know it was Phil. What irregularities? Was it just more of his games? "Sorry, that's my work," Liz said, already turning to her car. "Are you sure you don't mind taking that bag in for me?"

"No worries. Thanks again for your help."

Chapter 25: Mary

Thank God, Captain Picard, the Golden Girls and a whole planet of ewoks that breakfast club exists, Mary thought as she watched her children hurry into the school before half past eight. She had already dropped Lauren off at her mum's for a day of baking and who knew what, and now she was free.

Despite her initial misgivings, she had to admit that the whole Wronged Women thing was proving to be pretty exciting. Normally if she got a morning free – a rare occurrence – she would spend it curled up on the sofa, watching trashy TV and eating the secret stack of chocolate she kept on top of the kitchen cupboards so that the children couldn't reach it. While feeling guilty about not doing any housework. Instead, on this particular Monday morning, Mary was going to meet Bernie's niece Alice to collate their notes on a genuine murder case. And feel a little bad about the housework. Still, no reason to think about that now and ruin a nice cosy chat about a brutal murder.

"I've got us a seat at the back," Alice said ten minutes later when Mary turned up at the café. She pretended not to notice that the girl had stubbed out a cigarette as soon as she'd seen her coming.

"Great. I brought my laptop."

Alice wrinkled her nose when Mary pulled it out of her bag and set it up on the table. "Is it steam powered?"

"Hey, it's not that old."

"Uh huh. Do you want a cake?"

Mary thought sadly of her bank balance, which was teetering on the edge of minus figures.

"No thanks. I'll stick with the tea."

"I'm going to get a doughnut," Alice said and went back to chat to with guy at the counter. Mary took the opportunity to allow her laptop to load up the browser. Four pop ups and a virus alert later, the window came up. Maybe Alice had a point. It wasn't exactly speedy.

Alice returned with a giant pink frosted doughnut. Mary tried not to salivate.

"Want some? It's too big for me."

"Well, just a little," Mary said, unable to resist. There was a happy moment of silence as both women chewed on the soft sweet dough.

"Did you see the photos the police sent out?" Mary said, taking a napkin and wiping the crumbs from her lips.

Alice leaned forward. "Yep. Pretty crap, weren't they. I put them into my editing software and tried to make them a bit better. Want to see?"

"Of course!"

Alice smiled shyly at Mary's enthusiasm. "I'll ping them over so we can look on the laptop screen."

She did as promised and they both hunched over the screen. Three photos appeared, all taken from the pub car park. The original grainy-grey police shots were on one side and on the other was a full colour version, which reminded Mary of those colourized historical pictures you sometimes saw on the Antiques Roadshow.

"That's very clever, you know. How did you add the colour?"

"It's only a forty per cent accuracy," Alice replied. She pointed at the woman's coat. "It uses an algorithm to work out what might be the most likely colours. See here, this coat, the software has put it at beige, but it could be grey or cream. That's why the police wouldn't use this stuff. It wouldn't stand up in court, of course, but I thought it might be useful."

"It's better than useful," Mary said, her eyes flicking over the images. "It makes her seem real, somehow. I feel like if I saw her in real life I would recognise her from these."

"She's not one of the school mums then?" Alice asked.

Mary peered closer. "I… I don't think so. I mean, you can only see the right half of her face, but the hair isn't familiar. It's kind of shaggy, isn't it? I don't think anyone has that style."

"Could be a wig," Alice replied. "I mean, I watch some of these videos online where people make themselves up to look like anything. Catfish types. When I'm not studying, of course."

Mary felt her mouth quirk up at the corner. If Alice felt guilty about spending her time watching make-up tutorials then what would she think about the amount of cat videos on Mary's own phone?

"So you think it could be someone we know?" Mary asked. She stared at the face, wishing it would suggest something to her, but the pixels said nothing.

"As long as they aren't too tall. Sam Jones was only five ten and she's a couple of inches smaller than him. Not fat, but not skinny either. I mean, you could be her."

There was a moment of silence.

"Sorry, what do you mean by that?"

Alice's face fell. "Well, obviously it's not you. I wasn't suggesting that at all. But you're the right height, the right build, and with a wig... it wouldn't be impossible."

"But it could be someone like me. My age, build and things?" Mary was trying very hard not to be offended but she wasn't succeeding. After all, it wasn't like she had an alibi for Jones's murder, unless four sleeping children would count as witnesses to her lack of a social life.

"Sure."

Mary sighed. "You've just described most of the mums at the school."

Alice shrugged. "Sounds like as good a place for a suspect list as any."

They spent the rest of the hour writing up the notes on the case so far, as well as preparing the files on the Weston case that was looking, to Mary's untrained eye at least, like a bit of a washout.

Eventually, Alice stood up. "I better go. I've got college after lunch."

Mary checked the time on her phone. "We've been here for two hours! I didn't realise."

"Time flies when you're solving crimes," Alice said with a grin.

"Is that what we're doing here? Doesn't feel like we're making that much progress."

"It never does at first. I remember when Auntie Bernie took this case about a missing lad in Glasgow. He was fourteen, stayed out overnight, didn't come home. The usual thing. We don't normally do those sorts of cases as nine times out of ten they turn up after a few days. But this lad wasn't the sort of kid you would expect to disappear. Kind of geeky, never missed a day of school, not a drinker, well-off middle-class family. Anyway, took us a full day of chatting to his friends, before we realised it was Comicon weekend over in Edinburgh. Off we went, proper road trip and found him after a couple of hours. Would have been quicker but he was dressed as a Stormtrooper and no one could see his face."

"Wow. I'd love to go to Comicon." Mary said, slightly forgetting the point of the story.

Alice sighed. "What I'm saying is, when we do these investigations, there's always that lull where nothing happens. Then before you know it you're bombing around an exhibition hall pulling the heads off superheroes to see who's hiding inside. Utter mayhem."

"I'll look forward to the mayhem then. Catch you later."

"You too."

Chapter 26: Walker

Never volunteer. Never say it's a quiet shift. Never buy a square sausage roll from a van on the side of the road. There were a few unwritten rules that police officers learned on day one. A fourth one might be never to bump into the Superintendent in the corridor when you've just grabbed three chocolate bars out of the vending machine.

"Constable Walker, isn't it?" Superintendent MacKinnon had a posh Edinburgh accent and a fairly impressive ginger moustache.

"Yes sir." How on earth did he know my name, the Constable thought. This can't be good.

"I've just been in a meeting with DCI Shearer and DI Macleod. Rob speaks highly of you, he says you've done well with the secondment to CID."

"He's been a good teacher," Walker said, hoping that modesty would go down well.

"See that you keep it up then. I had a look at your file."

"You did?" Walker wasn't sure whether to be pleased or worried. A constable didn't generally attract the attention of someone so high up, unless they had done something seriously wrong.

"You were in the army before you joined, is that right?"

"Yes sir, Five Scots."

MacKinnon smiled. "I was in the cavalry myself, a long time ago now. Good to see another veteran in the force. You keep your nose clean and you'll do well here. Although, next time try something healthier for breakfast, won't you?"

"Yes sir." Walker sagged with relief when the Super hurried off down the corridor. He hoped he hadn't done his chances of promotion any harm with a lapse in nutritional judgement.

"You're well in there then," Sergeant Neil Michelson said, with more than a trace of envy in his voice. He'd appeared from a nearby office, clearly lugging into the conversation. "Army old boys' network and all that."

Walker laughed. "Maybe if I'd been an officer like MacKinnon. Don't think they care much about the grunts like me."

"Well, whatever happens, he knows your name now. Could be good, mind you, but you better not screw up."

"Thanks."

"You're welcome."

Neil wandered off and Walker watched him go. Are we going to have a problem here, Sergeant, he wondered. Walker would rather not have to deal with a guy with a chip on his shoulder about the army thing, but it wouldn't be the first time. Some police officers seemed to think it gave him a head start, but the truth was that if he'd joined the force ten years ago rather than ruining his knees in some miserable desert training camp, he'd have been much further up the ladder than he was now. Well, better late than never. If this case worked out he could be a Detective Inspector before he was forty. That was worth a little backchat from the rest of the guys.

"That you, Walker?" Macleod barked from the other end of the office as he walked into the room.

"Yes sir. I was just talking to the guys in IT. They've finally received the passwords for Jones's phone and laptop, so we're going to get something from them in the next hour. His social media accounts might take a little longer, but should be through by the end of today."

"About time," Macleod said. His chin was getting more than a hint of stubble and he wasn't looking quite as polished as when he had arrived. "The Super has just been telling me how important it is that we make an arrest in the next few days. Without, of course, offering me any more men. They're still needed up in Glasgow. Some big conference or another."

"The G8, I think," Walker said.

"Thanks, Tony Blair," Macleod snapped back.

"I don't think he's around anymore," Walker put his hand in his pocket. "Chocolate sir? If you don't mind me saying, you seem a little grumpy today. Might be your blood sugar."

"You're a cheeky bugger, you know that," Macleod said, grabbing a dairy milk and shoving it into his mouth.

"Yes sir."

"You can stop sirring me too. It's Rob in this room, all right."

"Sure," Walker said, even though he knew he would still think of him as Macleod. "And thank you for putting a good word in with the Superintendent with me."

"MacKinnon is a good guy," Macleod said. "Spends too much time on his spreadsheets, but he's fair. If you want to get your Sergeant's exam soon, keep on MacKinnon's good side. There might be an opportunity here soon enough. I heard that they're looking for a few new sergeants in this district over the next year."

"Well, I'd rather get back to Edinburgh," Walker admitted.

"Prefer city life, do you?"

"Yes sir."

"And you fancy a move to plain clothes?"

"Yes."

Walker let his eyes wander around the Inspector's office. Before the Major Investigation Team had moved in it had been empty and used to store supplies for the vending machine. It still had a slight scent of out of date crisps.

"Well, tell me something I don't know then. Impress me." Macleod's eyes twinkled with humour.

Walker drew in a breath. He was lucky he'd arrived early to do an interview first thing that morning. "Actually, there is something. I've just taken a witness statement from a woman that was in the bar on Thursday."

"Anything interesting?"

"Not really. Her name is Cheryl McConnell. She saw the victim, but not the woman he was with. She recognised him as they'd gone on a date a few months ago."

"Alibi?"

Walker nodded. "I checked. The CCTV shows her leaving before him on the night of the murder, so we can rule her out. But here's something I wasn't expecting. She says that two private investigators told her to contact the police."

"Private investigators? Please tell me we don't have any of those guys sniffing around this case."

"She said it was two women. Bernie and her friend, she called them. Thing is, that's the name of one of the women we caught snooping around Sam Jones's garden."

The Inspector leaned back in his chair, a small frown appearing between his eyebrows. "What's their game then? Playing at being detectives? Or could they be involved in the case somehow? Neither of them fit the description of our suspect, do they?"

"Not as far as I can see. I think it's probably just a case of... what was it you called it? The neighbourhood busybodies. But I thought I might find out where they were on Thursday night, just in case."

Macleod turned back to his laptop. "Good idea. Let's wait for the phone records, then you can pop into our local busybodies in the afternoon. Might even get a cup of tea out of them if you give them that winning smile of yours."

"Sure."

Chapter 27: Bernie

Sam Jones's murder was the most exciting thing to happen in Invergryff since Lacey Pirrie's boy burned down the old scout hut because they'd refused to take him on the ski trip to Austria. And even then it had been a short-lived excitement as the young lout had sprayed his own initials on the building before torching it, making it a nice open-and-shut case for the fire brigade. On Monday morning, however, there was only one topic of conversation in the playground.

"Did you hear it was some drugs gang over from Glasgow?" one younger mum told Bernie, her face pink with excitement.

"No," Bernie said. "Where did you get that from?"

"Oh, everyone's saying it. He owed them money. He was an addict!" The woman – she had one of those androgynous names, Bernie thought, like a Kayden or a Bailey or something – looked positively thrilled at the idea of her child's teacher having been killed.

"Addicted to what?"

"Well, drugs, I suppose." Having shown the limits of her knowledge, she scurried off to speak to another group of young mums all in sports leggings.

Not that any of them had ever as much as walked past a gym, Bernie thought. Could do with it too. If you were tending to the chubby side by thirty, it was all too easy to get out of control by forty. Just like she had done before she had had her epiphany. Well, they would realise that in their own time, she thought, although whether any of them would have the discipline to do anything about it was another thing. Not everyone could be a five star slimmer three months in a row.

Bernie noticed that one of the mums – was it Fiona something? Names were so hard to remember – was standing away from the others, sniffling into a handkerchief.

"It's just so sad that he's dead," she said when Bernie asked if she was all right.

Bernie raised an eyebrow. In all the excitement and gossip over the murder of the teacher, this was the first time anyone had mentioned being sad about it.

"He was a lovely, lovely man."

"Hmmn," Bernie was noncommittal, resisting the urge to say that he might have been a 'lovely' man but he hadn't exactly been a brilliant teacher. "Did you think so?"

"Oh yes. I asked him out once. For a coffee."

"So, you dated?"

"Oh no, he turned me down. Said no, but in a nice way. I'm not sure what I was thinking, only… you know how hard it is to meet men when you've got kids and he looked a bit like a young George Clooney, with nicer hair, so… I was gutted when he said no, to be honest, even though he explained it was just because he wasn't allowed to date mums of kids in his class."

Heavens above, Bernie thought, some women just needed to

get a grip. "Well, looks like you might have had a lucky escape," she said. "I hear that he was an addict."

"No!"

"That's what people are saying."

Fiona stood up a little straighter. "Ah, that's probably why he turned me down then. I don't even like taking paracetamols for PMS."

"There you are then. Much better to find someone more suitable. Maybe get your hair done, I hear that the Salon on Musswell road is doing twenty per cent off at the moment."

"My hair?" Fiona raised her hand to her greying roots.

"Must dash," Bernie said. She had just spotted the head teacher walking through the playground and she was determined to have a little word before school started.

Chapter 28: Bernie

"I understand your concerns, Bernie, but do we have to talk about the autumn pumpkin fun day right this second?"

Bernie crossed her arms. "Well, Mrs Figgis, I do think it's important to get these things sorted. The council has some very specific guidelines on music systems and nuisance noise."

If Bernie had been the sort of person who went in for introspection, she might have felt a little ashamed at putting more strain on a flustered Mrs Janice Figgis. Even on a normal school day she had the look of someone permanently searching for something when they have forgotten what the something is.

Today, unsurprisingly, Mrs Figgis looked more bewildered than usual. Bernie wondered if she should inform the woman that her blouse was on inside out.

"Just a few minutes to go through the forms," Bernie said firmly. "I can submit them all for you if you like, save you a bit of time. I had to do them for the care home's annual tombola last month."

"Oh, that would be a great help. We are rather short staffed at the moment."

"Ah yes, the unfortunate Mr Jones," Bernie said, as if that wasn't why she had accosted the woman in the first place.

"Of course, it is a terrible tragedy, but I cannot help wishing that he had uploaded this week's lesson plans. The supply teacher is going to have a terrible time."

"Not to mention the disruption that the investigation is causing," Bernie added.

"Do you know I had two policemen come to my house? Can you imagine?"

"That must have been very upsetting for you."

"It's not as though I could tell them anything. Sam Jones kept to himself. He didn't socialise with the other teachers. Some of the younger staff members, you know, they like to get together, go on nights out to Glasgow, that sort of thing. Sam never seemed interested in that. He got his hours done, then he went home."

"You didn't like him, then?"

"I didn't say that. He was very modern in his methodology, but no one has ever accused me of being old-fashioned."

Not to your face at least, Bernie thought. "And there were never any issues with the other teachers?"

"I hope you're not suggesting anything improper. The staff know how I feel about relationships within the workplace. No, there was never a hint of anything like that."

But would Mrs Figgis have known if anything had been going on? Probably not. She was nearly at retirement age, and if there had been a fling between her younger staff members, Bernie couldn't imagine any of them confessing anything to the head.

"I have to meet his sister in an hour," Mrs Figgis said, rearranging the towering pile of paperwork on her desk. "Goodness knows what to say to the woman."

"I didn't realise he had a sister?"

"From down south somewhere. She's the next of kin, poor thing. The parents are a bit elderly, so the girl has taken on that role. Must be terrible for her."

"I don't suppose you caught her name?"

Mrs Figgis gave Bernie a sharp look. "Why would you want to know? I do hope you won't be gossiping with the other mothers about all this."

"The very idea!" Bernie said, standing up from her chair. "I'll get those forms sent off for you today. Don't you worry, the success of the turnip carving is in safe hands."

"I thought it was a pumpkin fun run?"

"That too," Bernie said, heading for the door. "That too."

Chapter 29: Liz

Monday was already nearly gone and Liz had hardly gotten through any of the work Phil had given her. She had already messaged her mum to ask her to pick up Sean. Again. Nanny hadn't sounded happy on the phone, and Liz knew she would be hearing all about it when she got home.

Her office phone rang.

"Liz? It's Mr Oliver from upstairs. Have you got a minute?"

The head of European Operations might have been 'Ollie' to Phil, but he was Mr Oliver to Liz.

"Of course. What can I do for you?"

"There's an issue with the Bloom file. Did Phil mention it?"

So that was what the text had been about. Liz had ignored it, thinking it was probably Phil winding her up. Yet another mistake.

"He said something about an irregularity, but I was prioritising the West beach project."

"Ah, is that not done yet? Well, could you spare a quick minute to see me in my office? Only if it's not going to be any trouble."

Mr Oliver's voice was likely a kindly grandfather on some American sitcom. Liz wondered if he practised it so that no one could tell that he was a total arse.

"Sure. I'll come right up."

At least Mr Oliver was on a separate floor from Phil. Liz could even take a different stairwell so that there was no chance of bumping into him.

"Liz Okoro, my favourite team member, in you come." Dazzling white teeth and a suspiciously brown tan for someone who lived in the West of Scotland, Mr Oliver oozed money from every pore. He had been given shares in the company when he joined in the early years, and they had worked out nicely for him. He could even afford two expensive ex-wives, if the office gossips were to be believed.

"You wanted to talk about the Bloom file?" Liz said, taking a seat opposite him. She knew better than to engage in small talk. Keep it professional. She couldn't afford another disaster like Phil.

"I've been very impressed with your work this quarter. The way you pulled together the figures for the audit, that was above and beyond the call of duty."

"Thank you." She had spent that entire week working until midnight, missing one of Sean's football matches in the process. He had scored his first penalty.

"I'm afraid though this Bloom report is not up to your usual standard. I got Phil to check it through and he agrees."

Liz frowned, trying to remember what had been in the report. Bloom holdings was one of their repeat clients, and the documents were normally quite straightforward.

"Can I have a look?"

"Of course. I'll bring it up on my computer." He typed with two fingers, she noted, despite the very expensive custom keyboard.

"I'm sure we can get this sorted quickly. I know that I and the partners have never had a problem with your work before. You know you're not here for the diversity ratings, don't you?" Mr Oliver said with what he probably thought was a friendly smile. "We do actually think you're good at your job."

"I know I'm good at my job," Liz said, flashing her best smile to mask the urge to smack him across the face. The idiot probably thought he was being 'woke' or something.

"Well, yes." His smile faltered a little. Perhaps he had realised he was on thin ice. "The thing is, we've definitely found some irregularities in this file. If you take a look at this section."

Liz came around to look at the screen. She was prepared to be outraged, but when she glanced at the figures, she could tell he was right, there was something funny about the spreadsheet.

"Some of this data is wrong. It looks like it's from the previous year, but it's been entered into this year's form."

"Ah, a simple mistake then."

"Probably."

"And this is your spreadsheet, correct?"

Liz didn't like where this was going. "I made the original document, yes, but it's open to everyone. I'm pretty sure that I entered the correct figures."

"Pretty sure."

Liz ground her teeth together so that her fillings tingled. "I will check, of course."

"Of course you will." He closed down the computer and gave her another predatory smile. "Phil seems to think you're a key player here, and if you're okay by Philip Hornby, you're okay by me. A man with a five iron like that knows the wheat from the chaff, if you get my drift."

Reeling slightly from the mixed metaphors, Liz nodded. "Thank you. I'm glad I have your support." She gritted her teeth. "And Phil's."

Chapter 30: Walker

"I have the phone records!" Neil Michelson walked in brandishing the printed sheets like he had won the world cup.

Macleod bounced to his feet. "Is there a copy online?"

"Yes, I'll get it up on the screen. But I thought you might want a paper copy too."

"Good man."

The Inspector grabbed the printout from the other's man's hand and started to flick through them. Walker resisted the urge to loom over his shoulder and instead joined his colleagues in front of the smartboard.

"Right, let's get the text messages up first," Macleod said, pointing at the screen.

"Here we are, night of the murder. We've got two outgoing and two incoming messages from six o'clock onwards," Neil explained. "Before that it's just work stuff. It starts with a message from Jones: *We still on for tonight?*"

Walker stared up at the screen where the message had appeared.

"And that must be her," Macleod said, "*Yes. Dinner and drinks?* Is her number saved in his contacts?"

"No. And that's the first time it's appeared on his phone, no other correspondence."

"Damn. Okay, next."

Everyone in the room watched silently as the messages scrolled down.

I'll pick you up at eight. Wear something nice. ;.-))

"What's that after the 'nice'?" Macleod asked.

"It's not showing up properly on the screen," Walker said. "But I think it's a winking face emoji."

Macleod chuckled. "Smooth character, our Mr Jones. What was the reply?"

Neil scrolled down. "The unknown number again two minutes later: *Can't wait to see you.*"

"And that's it?" Macleod's shoulders sagged. "No name, nothing?"

"Not so far. But we've only just got into the phone, we've still got all the emails to go through, and we'll check if there are any dating apps, anything like that that might show us where he met her."

"Still no bloody name," Macleod muttered, zoning out of the conversation. "The Super is going to love this. What information have you got on the date's number?"

"Not good," Neil replied. "It's one of these online text message sites. You can send texts that look like they're from a mobile, but they're not."

"Well. That does suggest she was planning something, doesn't it. I suppose it's untraceable?" Macleod rubbed his chin.

"Pretty much. I've got the IT crew on it, but they don't sound hopeful."

"Did he access his phone at all during the date?" Walker asked.

Neil shook his head. "As far as we can tell, the last time he checked his phone was at seven-thirty. He checked his messages and a news website. That's all."

"All right Neil, let's work on the phone and the laptop. Go back six months and see if there's any hint of our mystery woman. Or anyone else for that matter. And if I sound like I'm bloody desperate, it's because I am. We're four days and counting since the murder and we've got nothing. Let's change that by the end of today."

Each member of the team trudged back to their desks. Walker knew that they had been hoping for something better from the phone messages. He had too. The case was starting to get an air of failure around it. They had made little progress since that day he had found Sam Jones dead in his car. Walker fired up his laptop. He needed a breakthrough. If this case turned out to be a disaster, it might set him back years in his plan to become a detective, and that was simply unacceptable.

After five minutes of scowling at his laptop, Macleod pushed his chair back and stood up. "I'm going to interview the rest of the school. The Head didn't tell us anything, but some of the other teachers must know more about Jones's social life. Neil, you're with me."

Walker tried not to show his disappointment. As he walked past Macleod put his hand on his shoulder.

"After all, the Constable already has plans. He's going to be interviewing our school mums and find out why they're playing at Miss Marple."

"Wow, a hot date with the leggings brigade," Neil gave his ribs a friendly jab.

"Shut up," Walker said, trying not to laugh.

"Aye," Macleod held up a warning finger. "It's not a joking matter. One of these harmless middle-aged ladies probably killed our victim. So keep your wits about you."

"Yes sir."

Chapter 31: Mary

"I thought we were only meant to have half an hour of screen time a day, mum," Vikki said, her nose creasing up in annoyance. "You've been on for an hour."

"Screen limits don't apply to mothers," Mary replied, giving her daughter a quick hug. "But nice try. Let me guess, you were wanting games?"

"Just a quick shot. I was really good at school, and Peter didn't even get any time-outs today."

Mary closed down her tabs and spun the laptop around. "You're right. For that minor miracle, you can both have half an hour each before dinner."

"Yes!" Vikki punched the air and her brother appeared from nowhere to join her. Within seconds they were bickering about whose turn it was. Mary shut the living room door behind them.

For a moment the house was actually peaceful. That is, if she ignored some sort of trampolining session going on upstairs where her two youngest were meant to be tidying their room. Maybe she would even manage a quick cup of tea before –

Greensleeves rang out in a tinny electronic tone from the hallway. I must work out how to change the doorbell, Mary thought as she walked to the front door.

"Hello, it is Mary Plunkett, isn't it? I was wondering if I might have a word."

She had been expecting a visit from the police since their little intrusion into Sam Jones's garden. At least she was prepared, thanks to her early screen time activities.

"Come in. I'm sorry I can't remember your name."

"Constable Owen Walker."

Walker, it sounded like something out of Lord of the Rings. He had the sort of rugged good looks of a hero in a fantasy novel as well. Well, so had Matt, and look how that had turned out, Mary reminded herself.

"Please ignore the mess," Mary said quickly, picking up discarded jumpers and shoes and trying to put them into a slightly neater pile.

"Don't worry about it," the police officer said, although Mary noticed he was being careful not to touch any of the furniture.

"I'll make you a cuppa. What do you take?"

"Just milk please."

The kitchen felt even smaller with Walker's large frame pressed against the counter. He was over six foot tall, and he looked like he would rather be somewhere else.

"What is that smell?"

Mary bristled. "It's a Mexican bean stew. Four of your five a day."

"Of course. Smells… great."

144

She couldn't help but crack a smile. "Maybe not, but it tastes good if you put enough chilli sauce on it. And it's healthy, so that's the main thing."

"You like cooking?"

"I've always loved it. It's my time to relax. Of course, it can be a bit annoying when you spend hours making stuff that the kids don't eat, but it's one thing that I'm actually quite good at." As opposed to all the other things that I'm failing miserably at, Mary thought, fishing some crushed tea bags out of the bottom of the bag.

"I like eating," the Constable said. His right cheek had a tiny dimple that only appeared when he smiled.

For a moment, Mary forgot what she was doing, then the kettle clicked. "I'll get that tea for you."

She peeked at PC Walker's reflection in the cabinet glass. Wasn't it one of the things that happened as you got older, policemen started to get younger? This guy was definitely younger than her, maybe not even thirty. And wasn't it weird how the uniform made anyone look handsome? That and his eyes which were the most extraordinary combination of hazel shot through with a touch of green.

She dropped the teaspoon and it clattered in the sink.

"Everything all right?"

"All fine!" Bloody hell, Mary thought, why does it have to be now? Six months since I left Matt behind in Aberdeen and this is the first person I fancy, and he's probably going to arrest me. Just my luck.

"I don't need sugar if you can't find it."

"Don't worry, I've got it!" She handed over the mug and he took it gingerly.

"Thanks."

DC Walker was giving her a weird look that Mary couldn't understand before she realised which mug she had used. It had a picture of Captain Picard saying 'Engage, tea!' while holding a cup of earl grey. It wasn't funny even if you were a Star Trek fan, and she had bought it in a drunken online shopping spree one night when she'd been bored and feeling nostalgic for nineties science fiction.

"So, you wanted to ask me about the case?" Mary said, determined to ignore the terrible mug.

"Um, yes." He took the tiniest sip of tea. "Actually, I wanted to check your whereabouts on Thursday night."

"Really? Are you asking everyone or is it just because I fit the picture." Mary was feeling rather offended to be told she looked like a murder suspect twice in one day.

"You don't fit the picture. You have short hair."

"I could have been wearing a wig."

Walker frowned. "I suppose you could have. Are you saying that you were there?"

Oh dear. "No, of course not. I just meant that someone like me could have worn a wig and they would look like the woman in the CCTV, that's all."

"Right. So where were you on Thursday night?"

"Here. Of course. Where else would I be?"

"And can anyone back that up?"

"Four people under the age of twelve. And Netflix. There's probably some internet history thing that would tell you I was watching stuff on streaming until about eleven, like I do every night."

"And what were you watching?"

Never lie to the police, Mary thought. She'd have to tell him that she was watching reruns of Supernatural, series seven, the one with all the vampires.

"A nature documentary and some science stuff," Mary said, her fingers crossed behind her back. "Just like I usually do."

Chapter 32: Walker

Constable Walker was finding the visit to Mary Plunkett's house more challenging than he had expected. And it wasn't just the tea that she'd made with some very questionable milk.

For one thing, he really didn't want to have to arrest a Star Trek fan. He'd spent most of his teenage years trying to grow a goatee like Lieutenant Riker. It hadn't gone well. For another thing, the woman was quite outrageously cute, with big pixie eyes and a great figure, albeit covered by a threadbare fleecy cardigan. Of course, he wouldn't have a problem arresting an attractive woman – he had always been professional about these things – but it was much nicer not to have to.

He wondered what the story was with the husband. She was a 'Mrs' after all, but there didn't seem to be much sign of him anywhere. Shame in one way as he could have provided her with an alibi for Thursday night. He would show her picture to the barman though, just in case.

"Something else I wanted to ask," Walker said, putting the cup down into the sink where she wouldn't see how little he had drunk of the tea. "I had an interview this morning with Cheryl McConnell who told me that she saw Mr Jones on the night he was killed."

"Is that right?"

"She told me you sent her to the station. That you'd already spoken to her about the case."

"Well, you're welcome, I suppose," Mary said.

Walker frowned. "I didn't come here to thank you. In fact, I came to find out what you're up to. You realise that this is a very serious situation."

The woman put her hands on her hips and scowled. Was that something that all mothers did? It certainly reminded him of his own mum when he'd done something wrong. He fought the urge to ask for forgiveness.

"You are not really journalists, are you? The website you mentioned doesn't exist. So why are you getting involved in this case?"

Mary shrugged. "We just thought we might be able to help."

Walker sighed. Busybodies, that was what Macleod had called them, and the Inspector had been right. "It's not like on telly, you know. If you're not a member of the police force, you shouldn't be going anywhere near a crime like this. It could be dangerous."

"You mean if the killer finds out that we're onto them and…" She made stabbing motions with her hands.

"No! I mean you could find yourself under arrest for obstruction! Seriously, Mrs Plunkett, this is not a game."

He expected her to apologise. Instead, she gave him a searching look. "Well, that's interesting. I did some research today on private investigators. It's amazing what you can find online. It turns out that you don't need a licence at all, even though they were meant to be passing a law in 2014. Looks like the government are running behind, as usual."

"Of course, I knew that," Walker said, feeling more than a little disorientated. People didn't normally quote legislation at him. Not when they had an 'I cleaned my teeth today' sticker stuck to their elbow. "I just meant that if you interfere in a police case —"

"It would be wilful obstruction, i.e. preventing a police officer from carrying out their duty. That was another internet search I did earlier. But surely sending Cheryl to you to give you her statement is the very opposite of that. It is, in fact, helping the police officer to carry out his duty."

Walker was getting seriously annoyed now. There was nothing more irritating than members of the public telling you how to do your job. And there was something wrong with the milk that felt like it was curdling in his stomach. "I am just here to give you some friendly advice. You and your friends should leave us to do our jobs in peace."

"Is that so?"

"I understand, it must be difficult for you, stuck at home all day with nothing to do."

The woman looked at him for a second, then pressed her lips together in a tight line. Too late, Walker realised that that might not have been the best thing to say.

"I just meant…"

"I know what you meant. You don't have children, do you, constable?"

"No."

"Well, let me tell you something, having nothing to do is definitely the least of my worries. Having just one second in the day when I *didn't* have something to do would be absolute bliss. You think we're just a bunch of bored housewives causing a nuisance, don't you?"

"That's not what I –"

"Well, that's what is going to make it even more embarrassing when we discover Mr Jones's killer before you do. Now, I think you should show yourself out, don't you?"

Chapter 33: Bernie

"I'm going to solve this murder or die trying!" Mary slammed her fist down on the table, almost knocking over the bottle of wine.

"Careful!" Bernie said, grabbing the bottle to stop it from wobbling. Truthfully, she was pleased to see meek little Mary Plunkett all fired up. Constable Walker had created a monster, and that was no bad thing.

"I mean, if you could have seen the arrogance of the man!"

"I think policemen are meant to be arrogant," Alice said, looking up briefly from her phone. "Isn't it part of the job description, to tell other people what to do?"

"In my own kitchen! And I made him a perfectly good cup of tea as well!"

Mary settled into sulky silence.

"All right," Bernie said, taking to her feet. "If we are quite finished with all the dramatics, we can start this week's meeting."

"Isn't Liz coming?" Alice asked.

"She's got a work thing," Bernie replied. "Something more important than catching a killer, evidently. All right. First of all, Viv Weston and her uncle's will. Now, I had a little look around the house last night."

"You're becoming quite the trespasser," Mary said.

"Indeed. I had a good look around the whole place and no sign of a will. But I did find this. Alice, avert your eyes."

Bernie placed a box of items on the table. It was a large plastic storage tub, and it was chock full of the sort of specialist items that used to be sold in back alley shops but could now be found on every corner of the internet, often with free postage and packing. There was a lot of imitation black leather and shiny PVC.

"Is that… wow." Mary put her hand to her mouth. "I don't even know where that one is for! And it seems to be banana flavoured."

"It seems that Peter Weston and his young wife were into some rather adventurous sexual practices." Bernie was enjoying the look on Mary's face. As a nurse, it took a lot more than some naughty toys to shock her. "There were also some interesting pictures. Polaroids, in fact, and I didn't even know they still made those."

"It's retro, isn't it?" Alice said. "Where do you put this thing?"

"Don't put it on the table!" Mary squealed, "we eat off that!"

"I think you've seen enough," Bernie said, taking the box and its salacious contents and putting it back on the floor. "The pictures show that Peter and his wife spent plenty of quality time together. It looks like the arguments the neighbours heard were the sounds of let's say adventurous physical activities. Often involving rubber. I think we need to tell Viv that her uncle was more than happy to leave his money to the woman who kept him so well satisfied."

"I feel a bit sick," Alice said.

"Well, if you're still this active in your old age you might not feel the same. I could tell you some stories about the care home, believe me."

"Please don't."

Bernie laughed. "Okay. If we're all in agreement we'll call it a day on the Weston case. Which is good, because things are getting interesting with our local murder."

"Did you get a visit from the cops?" Mary asked.

"Not yet," Bernie said. She was feeling a little peeved that Mary Plunkett had had a visit and she had not. "Maybe they're leaving me until last as a seniority thing. After all, I've been doing this much longer than you have."

"Or maybe the Constable just fancied Mary," Alice said.

"Unlikely."

"Hey!"

"As far as we are concerned, the police are not to be trusted. Don't let them sweet talk you into giving up our secrets. Our livelihood depends on getting to the truth before they do."

Mary gave her a sullen look. "Well, it's not like we're actually getting paid for this one, is it?"

"No, but think what good advertising it'll be. Wouldn't you want to hire the sleuths that tracked down a murderer before the police did?"

Mary simply folded her arms and looked out of the window. Bernie was getting a little tired of all the attitude. Liz never argued with her like this.

"Let's focus on our next moves. I happen to know that Sam Jones's sister is in town, and I think one of us should speak to her."

"How do you know that?" Mary asked.

"From our head teacher. How that woman managed to pass a single exam is beyond me. She couldn't run a jumble sale let alone a school. Mrs Figgis told me that Sam Jones's sister was in town from 'down south', and that narrowed it down a bit. Woman with the last name Jones, and an English accent, not many of them about. Anyway, a good friend of mine knows all the cleaners that work the hotels around here and it only took a couple of calls to find out that she's staying in the Burnside."

"Is that the one that got shut down for cockroaches in the trifle?" Alice asked.

"No, that's the one where the old manager got done for flashing the OAPs that came off the cruises," Mary said, topping up her wine. "Don't you remember, he was wearing a maid's uniform at the time?"

"Could we get back to the case in hand?" Bernie said sternly.

"Of course," Mary said. "Please, go on. I'm writing it all down in the minutes for Liz."

"Well, turns out that Sam Jones's sister, Millie Jones arrived two nights ago. The police have already spoken to her, but we know that they miss stuff, so I'd like to have a chat with her."

"I can't do the next couple of days," Mary said. "I'll be at the meeting Thursday night, but I've got too much on with the kids before then."

"And I'm getting my eyebrows bladed," Alice said. "I won't be fit to be seen until the weekend."

Bernie looked up at the ceiling. She wondered if the police had to deal with this sort of nonsense. "Well, I can't do it. I'm working lates from tomorrow. I'll ask Liz. She owes us after missing tonight."

Chapter 34: Tuesday Liz

First thing on Tuesday, Liz had submitted the files to Phil a full hour earlier than she'd needed to. Never mind that she'd had to work all night on Monday to do it. It was done, and now she could turn off her phone for a couple of hours.

Perhaps a bubble bath, she thought, checking the time. She had an hour before she had to start thinking about picking up Sean from school, so maybe she could actually relax for once.

There was a buzz from her handbag. She reached over to her phone with the usual sinking feeling, but that left when she saw it was Bernie texting.

Can you meet Sam Jones's sister Millie at the Bankside Hotel today? Ask her about woman from pub. This was put to the vote last night and you were volunteered. Lol.

Damn, she really should have turned off her phone. Lol indeed. Bernie knew fine well how Liz felt about that place. Ah well, if this was her punishment for missing the meeting, it could have been worse. She picked up her keys and headed out to the car.

The Burnside Hotel was only a short drive away. It was an old building, from the late Victorian period when they seemed to build everything big and bold with turrets and decorative ironwork. Like the rest of Invergryff, it lurched from too busy in the summer, to too quiet in the winter. Now, as they were heading into autumn, it was starting to get the abandoned look that it would keep until the bus tours started up again in the spring.

Liz had been there once with her mother for an Afternoon Tea. The scones had been stale, and the teabags were from the local supermarket own brand range. Grace Okoro had had plenty to say about that.

There was some dreadful fake music playing when Liz walked into reception. The young girl behind the desk had a set of earphones in that she pulled out when she saw she had company.

"Sorry, I had a podcast on. True crime."

"Don't blame you," Liz grinned. "Better than listening to that rubbish."

"Management's choice, I'm afraid." The young receptionist shrugged. "I guess they think it won't offend anyone if it's not real music."

"A management philosophy shared by many, unfortunately. I wonder if you could help me, I'm here to see Millie Jones, could you let her know that I'm here?"

"Sure. Who should I say is calling?"

"She won't know my name. Can you tell her it's someone from the school?" Liz didn't even wince at the lie. She was getting better at channelling her inner Bernie.

Millie Jones came down the stairs in a smart two-piece suit that was only lightly crumpled. She was a brunette, maybe in her late forties with a face that was skinny, bordering on gaunt. There wasn't much resemblance to her brother, Liz thought, except maybe in the shape of her nose.

"Hello Miss Jones. I am so sorry for your loss," Liz said. Clichéd, but still the only thing there was to say in this situation.

"Thank you."

"I wondered if we could have a chat. Can I buy you a coffee?"

"There's a resident's lounge in the back," Millie Jones said.

"Perfect," Liz replied, although she would have preferred a chain coffee shop. You always knew what you were getting then.

Sure enough, the hotel coffee was stale, served by a teenager with an eagle tattoo on the side of his neck that looked more like an angry seagull. Maybe it was meant to be an angry seagull. People got all sorts of strange things inked on their bodies these days.

"You're from Sam's school? I already talked to the head teacher."

Time to come clean. "I'm actually a parent from the school. My son had Mr Jones as a teacher."

"Oh god, he didn't sleep with you, did he?"

Liz tried not to look offended. "No."

The woman put her hand to her forehead. "I'm sorry, it's just he could never keep it in his pants. Even when we were younger. He was always the cheeky one, chatting up all the girls. Poor sod. Look where it's got him."

"You think that's why he was killed?"

Millie Jones shrugged. "I know the police keep going on about the woman that he was with at the bar, but I think it's much more likely to be someone's husband. He liked the married ones, you see. He told me once that it was easier that way because there were no expectations."

"Wow."

"I know. He was my brother, but it wasn't like we were close. I hadn't seen him in almost two years. Of course, to my folks, he was always the perfect son. Our Sam, teaching the nation's little ones. So selfless. And maybe he was at work. But in his private life, he was… he was kind of a dick."

Millie rubbed her eyes. They were red-rimmed, and Liz could tell she was on the verge of more tears, even talking about how she didn't like her brother. Families. They were always a nightmare, no matter who you were.

"If you weren't going out with him, then why…"

"I'm trying to find out who killed him. My friend and I, we run an investigation service and we're helping the police to find out what happened." It was only half a lie, Liz thought, but the other woman didn't even seem to take in her words.

"Sure," Millie nodded, looking down at her hands.

Liz pressed on. "I guess you have no idea then if he was seeing anyone."

"I can tell you right now he was seeing someone. Probably multiple someones. But nothing serious, that's for sure."

"And he didn't get in touch with you to let you know that he was worried about anything?"

Millie shook her head. "No, nothing. Last I heard from him, apart from a text on my birthday, was when he bought the house. He was so pleased to have his own place, even though mum and dad must have helped him out. He was always pretty terrible with money."

"So you think your parents gave him money for the house?"

She tilted her head to one side. "I can't see how else he would have done it. When he lived in London he was only renting, and I know he had a load of credit cards. It's not like teachers are rich or anything."

"Do you think you could ask your parents for me? I mean, I wouldn't want to intrude on them right now."

"I guess so," Millie rubbed her face again. "I don't see why it matters so much to you though."

Liz leaned forward across the table. "If someone was murdered, someone who worked with your kids, wouldn't you want to know? We don't want anyone else to be killed. Not if there's a way we can stop it."

"Uh huh." Millie looked down at her shoes and Liz could tell she had zoned out of the conversation. She wondered if the woman had taken a sedative or something. She could hardly blame her. Grief was a difficult thing at the best of times, but no one had a script for how to deal with your brother being murdered.

"Can I give you my number?" Liz scribbled it down on the

receipt for the drinks before Millie could say no. "If you need anything at all, please get in touch. I know you don't know many people in town, so I'll be happy to help.

"I don't know anyone here at all," Millie said, closing her eyes. "Not now my brother is dead."

Chapter 35: Mary

It was Tuesday morning, there were four loads of washing to do and Mary was trying her best not to notice that she'd been talking to Matt for ten minutes and he hadn't asked about the kids.

"And then that Benjy from human resources said that I hadn't, in fact, paid the NI in advance as we'd thought."

"Right." Mary had always thought that the point of separating from your husband meant that you didn't have to put up with his rubbish anymore. Turned out you just got more of the boring chat with none of the occasional sex. Not exactly how she'd imagined it.

"And how are the little ones," Matt said, once the pause had become so long it was uncomfortable.

"Good." Mary poked her fingernail into the side of the couch where the fake leather was coming away from the stitching.

"They miss me?"

"Of course they do. But you're coming down next week, aren't you?"

"Aye, although I don't know if I'll manage the three days. Work, you know how it is."

"Okay." When she'd moved away – let's face it, ran away – Mary had told herself she would have an amicable relationship with Matt. That they wouldn't end up being one of those broken families where they bitch at each other about how little they see the kids.

But then he couldn't manage three days off when he hadn't seen the kids for a month?

"How long will you be down for then?"

"I'll be here for the Saturday and Sunday. 'Course I'll have to go up on the Sunday night."

"Sure. And you've booked into a hotel?"

Another awkward pause. "No room at your place?"

"Definitely not."

"I'm sure I'll work something out. I wouldn't want to cramp your style."

Mary did not rise to the bait. "Is there anything else?"

"Oh, I heard you got a new job."

A piece of fake leather came off in her fingers and she flicked it onto the floor. "You've been speaking to mum."

"She called me. Wanted to know how to program her new sky box, but I think she was fishing for information. I didn't mention anything about... you know."

"Good." Damn, Mary thought, she would have to tell her mother. And soon. Better it came from her than Matt.

"You've not told her then?"

"No. But that doesn't mean it's not happening, Matt."

"Sure."

Mary tried not to hear the hope in his voice.

"I heard you're doing some admin thing. Bit beneath you, isn't it?"

She sighed. "I've had ten years out of the workplace, Matt, I'm lucky to get anything. Besides, it's not just admin. Actually, I'm working for some private investigators."

"Investors in what?"

"No, investigators. Like, you know, detectives."

Mary was already blushing before she heard him chuckle down the phone.

"Oh come on. This is just like all those silly shows that you watch on Netflix. What are you really doing, Nancy Drew?"

"I've got to go," Mary said, stiffly. "See you next week." She clicked off the call before he could say anything else. She was still glaring at the phone a minute later when it started to ring. It gave her such a shock that she dropped it onto the floor, where it collected a half-chewed wine gum.

"What is it, Bernie?" Mary said once she had retrieved the phone and pulled off the offending sweet.

"You're a good cook, aren't you?"

"Not bad."

"Could you do a lasagne? Today?"

"I mean, I suppose I could. It would take an hour or so. May I ask why?"

"Because it's Geoff Bilsland's favourite dinner. I'll pick it up at two."

Bernie clicked off the call before Mary could ask who the hell Geoff Bilsland was and why he was so in need of a lasagne.

Chapter 36: Bernie

Say what you will about Mary Plunkett, Bernie thought as she hurried out of the woman's house clutching a foil-covered lasagne, the woman can cook. The smell of melted cheese and oregano coming from the package was making her mouth water.

"Are you coming or not?" Bernie called as she climbed into her car.

"Sorry, just grabbing the nappy bag." Mary hurried out, a wriggling child in one arm and a bag that might have contained enough supplies for a three week expedition in the other.

Bring her with us, Bernie had said, but as they went through the rigmarole of swapping the car seat over to her car and strapping the sticky little creature in, she was already regretting it. Then the kid started singing 'Twinkle twinkle, little star' at the top of her lungs.

"She's a hoot isn't she," Mary said happily, making silly faces at her daughter from the passenger seat.

"Sure is," Bernie replied, turning on the radio. Unfortunately, she couldn't have it up loud enough to drown out the child without making her ears bleed.

"I think I know where we're going," Mary said, checking the kid's seatbelt for the third time.

"Uh huh."

"You said Geoff somebody. That's the name of Sam Jones's neighbour, isn't it?"

"Bingo," Bernie said. "Good to see you've been paying attention. I had a little word with my friend Annie at the home. She was a teacher, you know. Knows every single person in this town. Well, she told me that Geoff Bilsland has hardly been out of the house since his wife died. He goes to the Legion once a week when the football season's on, but that's about it. Oh, and she told me that his wife used to make a mean lasagne. I'm hoping that your cooking will be good enough to get us in the door."

"No pressure then," Mary chuckled.

Plenty of pressure, Bernie thought, as Lauren launched into 'Five little ducks'. If I've had to listen to this screeching child for no reason I will sack Mary Plunkett myself.

"Here we are then," Bernie said as the car pulled up outside Sam Jones's house for the second time. "No sign of any cops either."

"Could be undercover," Mary said, looking around the street.

"Don't think they've got the budget for that," Bernie said, climbing out of the car. "Come on, bring the little one. If we're lucky Geoff Bilsland might like kids.

When the man in question opened the door and saw the three-year-old sticking her tongue out at him, Bernie thought they might have been unlucky after all. Then Mary stepped forward, proffering the foil-wrapped dish.

"Hello, Mister Bilsland, isn't it? We heard about your

neighbour, and we just wanted to pop by and see if you're okay. I was doing a little cooking, and I thought you might appreciate a warm dinner."

Bilsland sniffed. "Don't need any charity here."

"Of course you don't," Bernie said, making sure that her foot was blocking the door in case he decided to shut it. "You won't remember me, but I work in the home where your wife stayed, just before she passed away. She used to make a fantastic lasagne. Of course, this won't compare to hers but we thought it might cheer you up a little."

He paused for a minute, nostrils flaring as the savoury scent hit him. "I'd still rather you took that to someone who needs it," he said, with some reluctance.

Bernie was surprised to see Mary step forward and give the man a warm smile.

"I understand," she said, "and we aren't here to patronise you. In fact, we wanted to bribe you."

"Bribe me?"

"We're private investigators and we're trying to find out who murdered Mr Jones. Bernie thought if we brought you a lasagne we might be able to ask you some questions. We heard it was your favourite meal. Silly really. Of course, you're too clever to fall for that, but I thought you might want to help us anyway. No one else can."

Bernie watched in fascination. The woman actually batted her eyelashes at him! But somehow or other it seemed to work. Geoff Bilsland nodded.

"All right, you might as well come in. And pop that lasagne in the oven. I've not had my lunch yet."

Chapter 37: Bernie

Geoff Bilsland's home was full of stuff. It was only one small step away from becoming like one of those hoarder's homes you saw on daytime telly. There were shelves on every wall, full of dusty vinyl and paperback novels. It smelled like no one ever opened the windows.

At least it was clean, Bernie thought as she put the lasagne into the oven. No dirty dishes were left in the sink or used socks on the floor, like in some old people's homes she had worked in. She knew all too well how quickly people could stop taking care of themselves. While Bilsland chatted to Mary in the other room, she had a quick look in his fridge. Nothing mouldy, and a couple of ready meals for dinners. Good.

"It'll be forty minutes to cook, and you can pop what you don't eat in the freezer," Mary was saying as Bernie came into the room. Little Lauren was sitting on the couch, trying to pull the sequins off her flowery top. At least she was being quiet.

"I guess you want to know all about Sam Jones, do you?"

"Yes please," Mary said.

"And it's true what they said on the news? Someone murdered him?"

"On Thursday night," Bernie said. "The police haven't got a clue, and we were thinking we might help them along a little bit. You know what it's like in Invergryff: everyone knows everyone else's business. Who better to solve this thing than one of us?"

Bilsland bristled. "I hope you don't think I'm some sort of curtain twitcher."

"Not at all," Mary said in her most soothing voice. Bernie found it irritating, but it seemed to do the trick with Geoff. "In fact, we just want the sort of things any neighbour would know. When he went in and out, whether he had any visitors, that sort of thing."

"Well, I can't help you on the Thursday. It's my night to help out with the meals on wheels. I was driving the van."

"That's okay," Mary said, giving Bernie a glance that showed her disappointment. "Maybe you could tell us a bit about Jones in general. What sort of a neighbour was he?"

"Well, he was quiet enough I suppose. Didn't cause me any bother."

"Let his garden get into a bit of a mess though, didn't he," Bernie said.

Geoff nodded. "Aye, he was lazy in that way. I never saw him outside except for the odd barbecue in the summertime. Why he didn't just get a flat in town I've no idea."

"And did you chat to him?"

"Nah. Said hello, that sort of thing. To be honest, I didn't like him much."

"No?"

"He was a scoundrel, that man."

"You mean with the women?"

"I meant in every way, but sure. He liked women. Seemed like he would bring a different one home every week."

"Was there ever any regular ones?"

"Well, I know he was seeing Sharon from the shoe shop. But that was a couple of years ago now. She was terribly upset when he finished with her. That was just after he moved in here. I heard her wailing out in the street. A crying shame, that was, poor wee thing."

"Do you know Sharon's last name?"

"No, sorry. But as far as I know, she still works there. Used to be a Clarks, now it's something else but it still sells shoes. Across from the Turkish barbers."

"I know it," Bernie said, making a note on her phone.

"I could never believe that man was a teacher," Geoff said, "he had the morals of a sewer rat. And a gigolo to boot."

"Whassa a gigolo mum?" Lauren asked.

"We'd better go and let you eat your lasagne in peace," Mary said, scooping her daughter up out of the chair.

"Let us know if there's anything else you think of," Bernie said, writing her mobile down and handing it to Bilsland.

"Like what? It's not like he's going to get killed again," Bilsland said, shuffling back towards the kitchen.

"We'll let ourselves out."

Chapter 38: Walker

Constable Walker hadn't been to the gym in nearly a week and he was sure that his muscles were starting to dissolve. Not that he was a gym bunny or anything. No, he hated the place. But the adult who had once been a little fat kid called Shortbread Walker had never spent this long away from exercise since his early twenties. He was sure that his work shirts were getting tighter.

"All right ladies and gents, let's get you up to the smartboard," Macleod said, his usual dark expression a little lighter than usual. They all shuffled out of their seats. Walker noticed that everyone was smelling rather less fragrant than they were a few days ago.

"What is it, sir?" Neil called out.

"We've got a fingerprint match," Macleod said. An excited murmur went around the room. "I know, no one is more surprised than me. A fingerprint from the passenger door has come up a match with one of our samples from the school."

"Which one?"

"A teaching assistant. Niamh Devon. Can you get her picture up on the screen, Walker?"

Walker flicked through the school photos until he found the right one.

"I don't know boss," Neil said, squinting at the picture. "She doesn't look much like the CCTV picture."

"She could be wearing a wig," Walker said, remembering his conversation with Mary Plunkett. "I mean, we know that she was hiding her face."

"Possible. A bit Hardy Boys, but possible. Any other possibilities?"

Walker thought back to the car. "There are a couple of unknown prints, aren't there? I guess he could have just given her a lift home at some point in the last few days."

"Right. And it might turn out that that's what happened. But it's five days after the murder and we've got no other leads. Let's at least pull her in for questioning."

Something was nagging at the back of Walker's mind. "Did you say her last name was Devon?"

"Yes. Got something?"

"Maybe." He scrolled back through the passages of comments he'd been looking at on social media sites. "What about this, sir, there's a load of comments from a 'Devonlady89' on here. I mean it's a bit of a stretch but I had highlighted the name as one of the ones to look into."

"What sort of comments?"

"Hang on, I'll do a search for them all. Let me put them up on the screen."

There were nearly two dozen comments, all on this one RIP post that had been shared from the main page of the *Gazette*.

"Seems like a lot of comments from someone who's just a work colleague."

Walker scrolled through all the posts. They started off rather simply. The first comment was from the day they had announced Sam Jones's death.

RIP he will be missed xxx

Sam Jones was one of the good guys. Too young.

"What's going on with this message," Macleod said, jabbing a finger at the screen.

Don't talk about what you don't know.

Walker stepped forward. "That was in reply to a message yesterday afternoon. The original message said: 'another stupid sod drink driving'. We've had a few of them come up, I guess because we said he'd been found in his car."

"Amazing how the public gets so much right and so much wrong," Macleod grumbled.

"Well, Niamh didn't like that. As well as saying not to talk about what he doesn't know, she's left another two messages in reply to the abusive one: *RIP best teacher ever.* And then a slightly stranger one: *Fake news, RIP Sam.*"

"It's always a bad sign when people say 'fake news'" Neil said. "One step away from the loony bin."

"I think you'll find that the loony bin is not considered PC anymore, Sergeant," Macleod said with a raised eyebrow. "Still, there is something more than a wee bit odd about all these messages. Let's get Niamh Devon in for a chat right away."

Chapter 39: Walker

It was hard to believe that Niamh Devon was the same height as the woman in the CCTV footage, but the techs had placed them both at five foot seven. Since she'd been brought into the interview room she seemed to have shrunk by half a foot, her head tucked down low on her chest.

"Can you confirm your name and date of birth for the tape?" Macleod asked. The Inspector had already said he would lead the interview, but Walker was happy to have been brought in as the second officer. He had pretended not to notice Neil's annoyed face as they had left the office together.

The young woman said her name and her date of birth in a voice that was barely above a whisper.

"We have asked you to come in for questioning today regarding the recent unlawful killing of Sam Jones. Can you confirm that you knew the victim?"

Niamh nodded. "We worked together."

"And your role is?"

"I am a Teaching Assistant at the school."

"How long have you been working there?"

"Just over a year."

Macleod asked a few more standard questions to get Niamh to relax, although it didn't seem like it was working. The duty solicitor, a young man from Glasgow, chewed on his fingernails while she talked.

"And can you tell us where you were on Thursday evening?" Macleod asked.

"I was at home."

"Can anyone confirm this?"

She attempted a small smile. "My cat, Dean, but that's about it."

At a glance from Macleod, Walker pulled the CCTV photos from the file. "Are you suggesting that this is not you in these photographs?"

Niamh looked at them briefly, then looked away. "No. She had blond hair."

"It could be a wig," Walker replied.

"I don't wear wigs," Niamh said, a frown creasing her forehead.

"We spoke to the manager of the bar. He said that you could have been the woman in question." Walker didn't add that the barman had not exactly been sure about it. He had said it could have been her, but he wouldn't even consider doing a line-up. It was flimsy at best, but it meant there was a possibility that Niamh Devon was the woman in the bar.

Niamh's already pale face turned whiter. "I... he must be mistaken."

"All right," Macleod said. "Let's move on. I want to look at

179

some evidence we've found on social media. Particularly regarding the death of Mr Jones."

Walker tried not to let his excitement show. He had spent the last couple of hours scouring the woman's social media accounts and he had finally come up with the goods.

"Do you post on social media under the name Devonlady89?" The Inspector asked.

Two pink spots appeared on Niamh's cheeks. "I can't use my real name, you know, because of working in the school. There's nothing wrong with that."

"Of course not," Macleod said. "It's understandable. Everyone is online these days, or so they tell me. It's the content of these messages that we were concerned about."

The Inspector pushed some printed pages across the desk to Niamh and her solicitor. "Here are some printouts of messages that Miss Devon posted after the death of Sam Jones. There are nearly sixty altogether across different websites. Don't you think that's a lot, Miss Devon?"

She looked to her lawyer. "No comment," she said softly. Walker tried not to show his frustration. There was nothing worse than an interview that turned into a constant stream of 'no comments'.

"In many of these messages, you express regret at the death of your colleague."

"Of course I did."

"But I would say that they go beyond what one might say

about someone you didn't know very well. For example, there are several messages here that express a personal sense of loss."

Niamh said nothing.

"My Constable here wanted to see if the username Devonlady89 had been used before online at all. He found some interesting posts from around six months ago. They appeared on a forum called 'Top Ten Teachers', a site which allowed people to say what they really thought of their teachers, which has since been deleted. Of course, nothing is erased once it has been online. Why don't you take us through the messages, Constable."

Walker leaned forward. "A user called Devon_lady_1989 appeared on this forum and posted a number of topics about Sam Jones all in the spell of two to three weeks. In contrast to your other messages, these comments are uniformly negative about Mr Jones. I've printed the full list here, but here's the highlights:

Mr Jones: Worst teacher ever

Mr Jones spends more time flirting with the mums than teaching the kids

Invergryff teachers are the laziest ever

Mr Jones is a disgusting sleaze

I suppose I am wondering what made you write these things, Miss Devon."

"It was months ago. I didn't mean any of it. It was just..." Niamh rubbed at her eyes.

"What did Mr Jones do that annoyed you so much?" Macleod prompted. "It must have been something pretty serious. You were risking your job by posting these comments."

"He… He didn't do anything."

Walker could have sworn that she was about to say something more, but she bit down on her lip as if to stop the words from coming out.

Inspector Macleod had seen it too. "You're not formally under arrest, Miss Devon, but we do need an explanation for these messages or we will have to take it further."

Niamh looked imploringly at her solicitor, who shrugged.

"Seems like someone venting their frustration online." The young man said. "You know how these things can be taken out of context. You still don't have the physical evidence to link my client to the crime."

"We have a fingerprint."

Another shrug. Walker was starting to hate this guy.

"Miss Devon has already explained that Mr Jones gave her a lift home the previous week."

"And she's sticking to that story?"

Niamh Devon inclined her head in agreement.

"For the tape, Miss Devon has indicated her consent. There is one more thing. With the physical evidence of the fingerprint and the messages, we were able to obtain a warrant to look at your laptop. Your personal one, not the school one."

"Oh god." Niamh put her hands over her eyes. If she had ever played poker, she would have lost a fortune, Walker thought.

"We found several thousand photographs. All of Mr Jones. Many were taken at the school, but some from outside his house. All seem to be taken without his knowledge."

Walker placed the damning printouts on the table. Sam Jones was in every picture, often turning away or in partial view. They had clearly been taken without his knowledge or consent. The solicitor swallowed, his Adam's apple bobbing up and down in his thin neck.

"Could I have a moment with my client," he said.

Niamh sniffed back a sob. "I wouldn't kill him. I loved him."

"You were stalking him."

"No! I mean, I was working up to asking him... I just didn't know how to do it. I would never have hurt him."

Macleod's jaw clenched. "Miss Devon, I'm arresting you on suspicious of the wrongful killing of Sam Jones."

"No!"

"Constable Walker, please read Miss Devon her rights."

Chapter 40: Mary

Mary could tell that Bernie was annoyed that she couldn't be there to interview Sharon from the shoe shop. However, Mary's mum had taken the kids to a soft play after school – otherwise known as the third circle of hell – so she had a couple of hours free. Bernie had fully intended to come along but there had been some drama at the care home.

"Bloody bingo day, always ends in a barny," Bernie had muttered somewhat enigmatically before barking off a series of questions that Mary should ask their newest suspect.

Was Sharon a suspect? Mary couldn't help thinking of her as one. It wasn't as if they had very many others. So far they hadn't exactly discovered a lot more than the police had. Less, if you were going to be technical about it. Mary thought about Constable Walker's smug face. Wouldn't it be nice to show him just how good they really were? All right, she had only been a private detective for about five minutes, but how hard could it be?

When she arrived on the High Street and found the address, it didn't seem like the sort of place a murderer would inhabit. The shoe shop looked like it had been there forever, under several different names that were just about visible under the current printed sign. It wasn't somewhere Mary would normally shop in. The styles on display in the window suggested a rather more elderly clientele. The slippers did look very cosy, though, she thought. Might save the heating going on for a while yet.

A bell jangled in a satisfying way as she pushed open the door. The first thing that surprised Mary was that it was quite busy. There was a woman in her seventies being helped into a pair of winter boots while sitting on a precariously tiny stool, and a couple of very elderly ladies who seemed to be having a good gossip in front of the reduced sandals.

"Be with you in a minute petal," someone called from the back. Mary used the time to investigate the prices, which seemed eye-watering compared to her usual supermarket purchases. As she stared at the discreet price tags, something in the shop was nagging at her. It was a rather terrible smell. Was it someone's feet? Mary tried not to look too suspiciously at the lady trying on boots.

Then there was a whimper from somewhere near her feet. It was a dog. One of those elderly ones that you smelt before you saw them. It didn't seem very hygienic in a shoe shop, somehow.

"Can I help you?"

"Um, yes." Mary looked down at the tiny woman with the blue rinse that had a 'Manager' badge proudly pinned to her suit. "Can I speak to Sharon please?"

The woman sniffed. "She's busy just now. And she's not allowed personal visits when she's on company time."

"Of course. Could you let me know when her break is?"

The woman rolled her eyes. "She normally goes out for a ciggie in about five minutes. You alright to wait outside? Only the lunchtime rush will be on in a minute."

Making sure to exit before the upcoming stampede, Mary spent a chilly ten minutes outside before a woman in her thirties walked out of the shop.

"Sharon?"

"Aye. Who are you?"

Mary still hadn't quite worked out how to answer that question. "I work for someone investigating the death of Sam Jones."

"You're not police though. No badge or silly hat."

"No, not police."

Sharon took a long drag on her cigarette. She was pretty enough, a bit too much make-up for Mary's taste, but she had the sort of figure that men like Jones liked. All boobs and bum. "You're not one of them tabloid journalists are you?"

"No."

"Pity. I was thinking of selling my story. Do you think I'd get much for it?"

"I'm afraid not. But I'll buy you coffee and a cake at the café over there if you'll talk to me for five minutes."

"Well, I'm only supposed to be having a quick ciggie, but if it'll piss off boney old Maggie then I'll do it. And it's a tea I'll have, not a coffee. And one of those chocolate eclairs. I'm on Atkins and they're practically low carb."

Mary bought the drinks and cakes, adding a slice of walnut loaf for herself. She made sure to keep the receipt: hopefully

Bernie was as good as her word regarding expenses.

Once they had found a table outside so that Sharon could smoke and keep an eye on 'that old hag', Mary brought out her notepad.

"According to our sources, you went out with Sam Jones."

"Aye. For about six months. This was two years ago, mind, and I've not seen him since."

"You didn't keep in touch?"

"Do you keep in touch with any of your exes? I didn't want to see him again. He was a prime tosser, even though you're not meant to speak ill of the dead."

"How did you meet?"

"Dating app. I don't even like them, but that's how my sister met her husband, so I thought, why not give it a go? This'll give you a laugh, his username was Sexysam87. Thought a lot of himself, he did. And as for the eighty-seven, maybe in his dreams!"

"Why did you break up?"

"Couldn't keep it in his pants, could he? He wasn't even subtle about it. I'd catch him looking at other girls on his phone, hiding it when any text messages came in, that sort of thing. It was the bare-faced lies that really pissed me off."

"Like he was taking you for a fool," Mary said, not needing to imagine the feeling.

"Exactly. It wasn't like I was looking for a ring or anything, but we had been going out for six months and he was treating me like a casual hook-up. No, I had to end it."

"So it was you that broke up with him? Not the other way around?"

Sharon coughed. "Well, I would have broken up with him. I'd been planning it for weeks actually. Then one night he tells me it's over. We'd just spent the night together, of course, he wanted to have one last shag before he ditched me. Then quick as you like before I'd even had my morning cuppa he asks me to leave. Well, can you imagine? I was so pissed off. I told him, you don't get to dump me, I'm dumping you!"

"You were angry with him?"

"Totally pissed off." She took an angry bite of her éclair, chocolate coating her mouth. "I didn't kill the old fool though, did I?"

"No?"

"I might have been annoyed at the time, but it's been years. As I said, I haven't even seen him since then. And it wasn't like I was upset. I think my dad was more bothered than I was. He always liked the idea of me having a man about the house."

Mary finished off her walnut loaf, which was a bit of a disappointment, as these things so often were. "The police will want to know if you had an alibi for Thursday night."

"What, do you think I killed him?"

I'm not at all sure you didn't, Mary thought. "No, no. I just mean, it's the sort of thing that the police ask isn't it?"

"Aye. They already did."

"What?"

"Yeah, they came by a couple of days ago. Said they were looking up all his old girlfriends, just in case. Well, lucky for me I was working in the chippy with my sister. The Fish Plaice, do you know it?"

Mary shook her head.

"Best batter in Invergryff. Kitty and her husband own it. She used to have just the one shop in Oban but she opened up here a couple of months ago. I help out there a few nights a week. That's where I was when someone was murdering Sam Jones. Didn't finish cashing up until two in the morning."

"Well, that's that then," Mary said. "I suppose you better get back to the shop."

"I'll have another cigarette first. The old witch can't have a go at me if I'm bereaved, can she?"

Mary left her to it.

Chapter 41: Liz

"Something funny happened today," Dave said as he pulled the macaroni cheese from the oven. It smelled amazing, creamy and rich, like savoury pudding. Liz would need a little hot sauce, of course, but she could tell it was going to be good.

"Oh yeah, what?" she asked, stealing a piece of caramelized pasta from the edge.

"I had to pick up some flyers from the hotel where they're holding the next conference. Do you know it, it's the Bankside Hotel."

"The Bankside? I was there today! How funny is that? Did you see me?"

"I saw you coming out and getting in the car."

"Then why didn't you say something."

Dave portioned up the pasta onto three plates. "I guess I wasn't sure why you were there."

"It was for some WWC business. I had to interview someone." Liz saw her husband's shoulders relax. "God, you weren't worried that I was meeting someone, were you? Like an affair?"

Dave tried to look casual. "Of course not. Only, it was kind of weird. And you are on your phone a lot."

"That's just work," Liz said, ignoring the usual pang of guilt.

"Honestly, Dave, you know I would never have an affair."

He kissed the top of her head. "I guess I do."

"And if I was going to, I'd do it in a nicer hotel than the Bankside," Liz added, jumping out of the way when he flicked her with the tea towel.

"Sean!" Dave shouted and their son ran in, grabbing a plate and shoving forkfuls into his mouth.

"Not a race, darling," Liz said, trying not to mind that she sounded exactly like her mother. Before she had had time to clear half of her plate, her son was finished and back outside again.

"Doesn't he want pudding?" Liz asked. "There's some yoghurts in the fridge."

"He just wants to play football. I was the same at his age. Tell me more about this WWC case now that I know you're not having it away in the honeymoon suite." Unlike Bernie and the others, Liz had told Dave from the start exactly what she was doing on her Tuesday evenings. He wasn't the sort of person to judge anyone else's choices.

"We're looking into the death of that teacher, Sam Jones."

Dave whistled through his front teeth. "Wow. Didn't realise you lot went in for murder."

"Bernie's got a bee in her bonnet about it. Thinks that we've got better local knowledge than the police. She's probably right as well. Half of them have been shipped over from Edinburgh."

"Oh, Bernie is always right about everything."

"You wouldn't say that to her face!"

He chuckled. "Damn right I wouldn't. That woman scares me half to death. But I bet that I know something about the case that none of you lot do."

Liz raised her eyebrows. "And what's that?"

"They've arrested someone."

"What? When?"

"I'm surprised you don't know seeing as you're such an expert."

She narrowed her eyes. Dave caught sight of her expression and held up his hands in mock surrender.

"Sorry, I was only joking. They've arrested one of the teaching assistants from the school. Niamh Devon. Her next-door neighbour, Rikki, was in the shop today and told me. Mild glaucoma he has, but not getting any worse. In fact, I've got this new treatment just in from –"

"Niamh? They've arrested Niamh? Are you sure?"

Dave nodded.

Liz slammed her cutlery down on the table. "Then they're bigger bloody fools than any of us thought."

Chapter 42: Mary

"What the hell is going on?" Mary said. She had been in her PJs when Liz had phoned, and after begging her next-door neighbour – Mrs Spencer who owned seven cats and believed in the healing power of crystals – to watch the kids, she had thrown on a jacket and a pair of boots and ran out of the house.

"Wait until we get Bernie," Liz said, glaring at the front door and waiting for it to open. "I need to tell both of you. You're not going to believe it."

"We didn't even bring any snacks," Mary said. There was a distinct absence of bottles of wine as well. This was not the WWC that she had come to expect.

Just when Mary thought that Liz might spontaneously combust with excitement, Bernie and Alice barrelled through the door.

"This better be good," Bernie said, taking off her coat. Somehow she was still in an uncreased blouse and smart skirt. Mary didn't know how she did it. "I was just about to sit down and watch Bake Off."

"I had a date," Alice said.

Everyone stopped for a moment and looked at each other.

"A date?" Bernie said. "I didn't realise you did dating."

"What, am I totally repulsive or something?"

"I suppose it's just that the idea of a date seems a little old-fashioned for someone your age," Bernie said, looking uncomfortable for once.

"Isn't it all online these days? Like, video calls or something," Mary said.

"Or sexting," Liz said with a nod. "Dave tried it once. I don't think we were doing it right though as we –"

"Can we just get on with it?" Alice asked.

"Yes, what is all this drama about," Bernie added.

"Here's the thing." Liz took a deep breath. "They've only bloody well gone and arrested Niamh."

Liz's expression was apoplectic with rage. Mary had only seen that written down before, and it was quite something to witness in the flesh.

"Um, who is Niamh?" Alice asked.

"From the school. Mousy little thing. Wouldn't say boo to a ghost. Now your boyfriend over at the police station thinks she has murdered Sam Jones!"

"What?" Bernie yelled, just as Mary said: "Boyfriend?"

"That police officer that is always coming over and making eyes at you. Fine detective he is, as if that little thing could have killed a soul. She probably faints at the sight of blood."

"I always thought she was a bit of a wet lettuce," Mary said.

"Wet lettuce!" Liz laughed. "That describes her perfectly."

"I don't get it," Bernie said.

"It's a Terry Pratchett line, actually. It means she's kind of limp, like a wet lettuce."

"Terry who?" asked Bernie.

"Never mind," Mary said quickly. "Let's get back to Niamh."

"We need to storm the police station or something," Liz said. "Get her out of there."

"Listen," Mary said, trying to calm the woman down. "Just because you think she's what... mousy? Just because she's mousy doesn't mean she didn't kill him. We all know people who seem shy and reserved and then turn out to have one hell of a temper."

Bernie nodded. "Like old Father Rennet we had at the home. A priest, no less. Well, he was so softly spoken you could barely make out a word until he found out that Larry Fraighton was cheating him at dominos. He nearly wedged the double six somewhere the sun don't shine. We had to pull them off each other in the end. Never looked at the man the same after."

Mary blinked. "Right. Anyway, just because you thought Niamh was quiet, doesn't mean that she didn't do it, Liz. They must have some reason for suspecting her."

"Of course they do. And we're going to find out what. Don't suppose you fancy pumping that policeman of yours for information?"

"Definitely not."

"Then we'll do it the old-fashioned way," Bernie said, reaching for her coat. "A six pack of doughnuts and twelve sausage rolls."

Mary looked over at Liz. "Do you have any idea what she's going on about?"

"Never. But it's more fun that way."

Chapter 43: Bernie

Mrs Battaglia didn't seem overly pleased that four women had turned up on her doorstep at ten o'clock at night.

"Jesus, Mary and Joseph. I thought you were the council, coming to complain about our Tam and the hot tub."

"Ooh, a hot tub, I've always fancied one of them," Mary said.

"Don't bother. Costs a fortune to heat and then the neighbours start complaining about seeing your husband in his speedos. I mean, old Mrs Wilton is eighty-four, you'd think it would be a nice treat for her."

"You would think so wouldn't you," said Bernie, even though she had seen Tam and couldn't imagine the words 'speedos' and 'treat' going together. "I've brought some little luxuries for you, from the shops, the usual bakery stuff."

"We could sit outside if you like," the woman said. "Tam's just finishing up, I was going to bring out his towel in a minute."

There was a resounding vote for staying inside, so the older woman led them through to the sitting room.

"Are the boys at home too?" Bernie asked, not really caring, but she needed to keep the woman on her side. Privately, she considered Mrs Battaglia's adult children in need of a severe kick up the backside.

"Nah, they're at the social club tonight. Poker night, I think."

Once the obligatory teas had been offered and accepted, Mrs Battaglia put her hands on her hips.

"Now Miss Bernie, I know you don't come here just for the Tetleys. What is it you are wanting?"

"There's been an arrest. In the murdered teacher case. But they've arrested the wrong person."

Mrs Battaglia nodded sagely. "Just like when I was a little girl in Naples. Always arresting the wrong person. Like when they arrested Nonna Greco's third cousin for running drugs from the harbour when everyone knew it was her second cousin, Franco."

"Just like that," Bernie said. "You didn't happen to see them bring the girl in, did you?"

"I wasn't in today."

Bernie felt her stomach fall. "I thought you always worked a Tuesday?"

"Not today. It's a Saints day."

The other women looked down at the floor and Bernie found she couldn't meet their eyes. "Well, I'm sorry to have wasted your time."

"Not at all. But if you're leaving, I don't suppose you would want to speak to her next door? Myleene? She covers my shifts when I'm off."

"And she's right next door?"

"Sure, number twenty-two."

Bernie stood up to go. "Thank you for your help."

"It's a pleasure," Mrs Battaglia smiled, showing them to the door. "And you can leave the sausage rolls in the kitchen."

After depositing two plastic bags with Mrs Battaglia – a rather expensive five minutes, Bernie thought – they went next door.

"Should we be ringing the bell this late?" Mary whispered.

"Mrs Battaglia said that Myleene works at a local café and doesn't get home until nine," Bernie said, pressing the doorbell. "She should be awake."

The door opened and a young woman who couldn't have been much older than Alice poked her head around.

"You'll have to be quiet. My dad's sleeping." The girl had a Govan accent and hair that was blond with pink streaks.

"You know who we are?"

"Mrs Battaglia texted me. Come on, we'll go into the front room. No one ever goes in there."

In fact, the front room was giving Bernie flashbacks to her childhood, with covers on all the sofas, porcelain ladies with voluminous dresses looking at them disdainfully from bookshelves, and coasters on every surface. The sort of room where children were never allowed. There wasn't much that intimidated Bernie, but she had to swallow twice before she could start her questions.

"We wanted to know what was going on at the police station today. Mrs Battaglia said you were working."

"Oh, I was there. It was very exciting. Not that any of them talk to me, but I see what's going on as well as the coppers do."

"Excellent," Bernie said. "If you could start with –"

"Mrs Battaglia said that you'd pay. Don't mean to be crass or anything, but it's me that'll get it in the neck if the polis discover I've been talking to you."

"Of course." Bernie nodded. "Alice, would you pop out to the car?"

"Why does no one use her first name? Mrs Battaglia I mean," Mary whispered into Bernie's ear.

Bernie shrugged. "I think it's an Italian thing. I don't even know what her first name is."

"Doesn't seem like an Italian thing. Maybe she –"

"Can we stick to the important questions please?" Bernie reminded her.

"Sorry."

Alice came back in with two bags for life. "I'm afraid the other lady took all the Gregg's stuff, but there are some nice Markies crisps in here, and some booze."

Myleene peered into the bags. "I'm not much of a drinker."

"Do you for Christmas though," Bernie said in a flash of inspiration. "There's two boxes of posh chocolates and some of that fizzy wine. Proper cava. Along with a case of beers."

"My dad will like them. All right, I'll talk to you. To be honest, my dad doesn't like me working in the cop shop anyway, after what happened to him in the eighties."

"Sure," Bernie said, resisting the temptation to ask for details. "Can you tell us what happened today?"

"Well, I was chatting to that Constable, you know, the hot one?"

"That would be Constable Walker," Liz said, digging Mary in the ribs. Mary was looking at the ceiling, trying to pretend she wasn't bothered.

"That's him. Bit old for me of course, but there's always something about a lush guy in a uniform, isn't there? Anyway, he's sat at his laptop and then he gets all excited, stands up and rushes in to see the big boss that has the office where I used to keep my hoover."

"Don't suppose you saw what was on the laptop?"

The girl gave Bernie a sly smile. "That would be a bit naughty wouldn't it? But if he just left the screen up rather than shutting it down, that wouldn't be my fault, right?"

"Right."

"He was looking at a bunch of photos of that dead teacher. They looked like they were taken when he wasn't looking, like when you see someone fall over and you take a pic to show your pals. They were all taken in the school."

"Maybe they were from Niamh's phone," Liz said. "I wonder why she would be doing something like that."

"Do you know, she did kind of follow him about," Mary said, her eyes squinting like she was concentrating on something. "I was picking Vikki up once from an afterschool club and she was just trailing after him, carrying his books and things. I thought it was a bit sad really."

"Do you think he was shagging her?" Alice asked.

"She seemed a bit wishy-washy for him," Liz said. "I mean, the other people he went out with like Sharon were all a bit more confident, dressed nicer, that sort of thing. I guess it's not impossible though."

Bernie nodded. "Not his type. Also, remember that he never dated any of the mums at school, so you would think he would avoid work colleagues too. No, I think we're looking at a one-way obsession."

"Unrequited love," Mary sighed. "So sad."

"And easily turned into hate, of course," Bernie added.

Liz folded her arms. "I still don't see how she could have done it. Yes, she could have moped over him, followed him about and all that, but taken him out to the pub and then bashed him over the head in his car? It just doesn't seem likely."

"He wasn't bashed over the head," Myleene said. She had opened one of the boxes of chocolates and was making her way through the fudges without offering them to anyone. "He was injected with something. I heard them talking about it."

"Really?" Bernie exchanged a look with Liz. "That does change things. An overdose administered by injection. Now that definitely doesn't sound like Niamh. Sounds more like something I would do."

"Excuse me?" Mary said.

"I mean, because I'm a nurse. Not because I'm a murderer."

"Clearly." Liz said, standing up to leave. "Thank you for all your help Myleene."

"No problem. Anytime you want to ask me anything, just ring the bell," Myleene said, picking bits of toffee out of her molars.

Chapter 44: Liz

Hell hadn't frozen over yet, but Liz had decided to take a day off mid-week. Her phone would be buzzing with messages the whole day, but she was determined not to let them bother her.

Last night Bernie had been making some not-so-subtle hints about Liz not pulling her weight with the WWC.

"You've not been pulling your weight," Bernie had said when Liz gave her a lift back from Myleene's house the previous night. "Even blooming Mary-not-so-contrary has been more on the ball than you."

"All right," Liz had replied. "I'll get back on the case."

She had felt kind of irritated by Bernie at the time, but now that it was the next morning, Liz could see her point. When they had been tracking down that young lad who had run off with the money from the charity tin, it had been her and Bernie together that cornered him on the number sixty-seven bus and made him give the money back.

Bernie probably felt abandoned. Her friend was the sort of woman that thought she could do everything herself, but Liz knew that wasn't true. Together they were daring detectives, tracking down criminals without so much as a police badge between them. On their own, they became just plain mums again. The WWC had given Liz the sort of satisfaction that had been lacking from her miserable job and she didn't want to lose it. Not without a fight anyway.

So she had messaged Phil and told him she was taking a holiday day for personal reasons and not even checked out his reply. And she'd picked up a family-size bar of chocolate from the corner shop for brain fuel. The day was looking promising.

I'm going to check out Sam Jones's work computer. Liz sent the text to Bernie, without knowing how she was going to do it.

She grabbed her coat and gave herself a thumbs-up in the mirror. Time for action. Liz opened the door, ready for the unknown.

And walked straight into her mother.

"What are you doing at home?" The woman said, her eyes narrowed.

"I took a day off. What are you doing here?"

"I came to borrow your big stock pot. I've got three sets of families from the Refugees' Alliance coming for dinner, so you can imagine I'm going to need a lot of rice."

"Right," Liz said, letting her mother push past her into the hallway."

"Will you put the kettle on?" Grace Okoro was pulling off her coat and scarf.

"Actually, I was just going out," Liz said, biting her lip to keep from yelling.

"Ach, you said you had a day off work. I'll take a proper brew, not one of those organic thingies you've been passing off as tea."

"Mum! I need to go and do something!" Liz tried not to notice that her voice had become a wail.

"What exactly could be so important?"

Liz breathed in through her nose, then came to a decision. "Sit down and I'll tell you. And you can make the tea if it's so important."

Ten minutes later Liz had introduced her mother to the concept of the WWC, and the older woman hadn't touched her tea.

"Well, I must admit I'm a little shocked."

"I know. It's not exactly what you expected of me," Liz tensed her shoulders, bracing herself for the inevitable criticism.

"But that's why it's so great," Grace said, her mouth changing into a grin. "You see, it was always your father that wanted you to get the dependable job. To make money, all that stuff. I mean, I did too, I suppose. When you grow up poor it's all you think about. Things were hard for us when we came over from Nigeria, and we didn't want you to have that struggle. But I think that without the struggle, you lost a little bit of that spark that I had to keep me going."

"Gee, thanks," Liz said, feeling her shoulders tense.

"It's not a criticism of you, it's a criticism of me. And your dad, of course. We worked so hard to make sure we would fit in here that we didn't think about what we were losing. I see you at that job of yours, trying to make sure that everyone likes you, working harder than all the white girls just so you can get the same respect they do automatically. And I understand, I do, but it broke my heart. And then when you said you were doing this detective agency thing… Well, it made me proud. That's what we used to do in the old days when we marched for black rights or helped other families coming in from Africa to get settled here. We were trying to stop injustices, of all sorts. And that's what you're doing, isn't it? The exact same thing."

For some reason, Liz's eyes were tearing up. "I suppose we are, in a small way."

"There you are then. You've found your spark, my girl. Don't you dare let anyone put it out."

"It's just… I'm just not sure that we're going about this the right way. We could get in a lot of trouble."

Grace Okoro took her daughter hand and gave it a squeeze. "Honey, sometimes you have to do a little wrong to make something right."

Chapter 45: Walker

It was eighteen hours since they had arrested Niamh Devon and the clock was ticking like one of those LED displays in an action film where everyone is about to get blown up. Constable Walker was hoping that a suave Englishman in a suit was about to turn up and save the day, but it didn't seem likely. Not in central Scotland during an early morning drizzle, anyway.

"What is it, Constable? You've got a face like a duck's bottom."

"You have a way with words, Inspector," Walker said with a laugh. He walked over to the Inspector who was collating interview evidence on his laptop. "I suppose I'm just concerned about the arrest. I'm not sure that Niamh Devon is the one we're looking for."

"As you well know, we have to follow the evidence and there's certainly enough of that to hold her for now. Her prints are in the car and she was clearly some kind of stalker. If we didn't arrest her we'd be negligent."

"But do you think she did it?"

Macleod sighed. "Honestly, I wouldn't rule it out. We don't know what happened on that Thursday night. He could have rejected her, said something that sent her over the edge. She might look harmless sitting in that interview room, but everyone has a point where they lose it."

Walker wasn't convinced. Yes, you heard of some surprising murderers in this job, but Niamh Devon didn't seem to fit the bill. But then, obsession was a dangerous thing and she was certainly obsessed with Jones. He didn't know what to think.

But something else was bothering him. "You know, sir, I'm not at all happy about this murder weapon. I mean a syringe to the neck? Sure, it's effective, but it's a bit amateur dramatics, isn't it? Most murderers just tend to stab their victim, or thump them over the head with something. The drug overdose seems so deliberate."

Macleod took a sip from his coffee, made a face, then added another sugar. "I've been thinking about it too. It's weird, and I don't like it when things are weird. It means that we're probably missing something obvious. Something that's going to get me a bollocking from the Super."

"Something that might mean Niamh Devon is innocent?"

"Sure. And if it's there we'll find it. But someone killed the teacher, and no one else is even close to being a suspect."

"Maybe we just haven't found them yet."

"Then get on it!" Macleod said, his voice raised. "After all, that's your job."

"Okay. Do I have your permission then to do some more digging?"

"Sure, if it'll get you off my back. I'll get Neil to work on the evidence to take Devon's case to the Procurator Fiscal. But we'll be charging her or releasing her by the end of today, so you're going to have to hurry."

"Right." Walker tried to sound more confident than he was. In reality, he had no idea where to start. So far, they barely knew anything about who might be responsible for Sam Jones's death, apart from the unfortunate Miss Devon. What he needed was someone with local knowledge. Someone who might share some information with the police.

Damnit, Walker thought, grabbing his coat. I only wish I didn't know who that is.

It only took fifteen minutes to drive to the school. Parking was impossible, of course, but he had the luxury of the police car so he parked in the staff car park. He checked his watch. Only ten minutes until school was finished for the day. The perfect time to catch his prey, except there was something strange tugging at his consciousness. Was someone singing? No, someone was chanting something.

He walked around to the playground and ground to a halt. Directly in front of him was a small group of women standing at the gate. This was where the noise was coming from. To his horror, Walker realised that they were all holding up homemade placards.

The collection of cardboard signs was all of a single theme.

Release the Invergryff One

Justice for Niamh

Black lives matter (which was crossed out with) *Let our people go!* (painted on top)

"Bloody hell!" Walker cried, earning a severe look from a teacher hurrying past with a stack of books. "Sorry."

Give me an 'N'!

"That's cheerleading not protesting," a voice hissed.

"Sorry Bernie," another replied.

With a sinking feeling, Constable Walker walked over to the women.

"Hello, face of oppression," Bernie said, giving him her finest glare.

"Bernie Paterson. And I don't think I've met you two?"

"Liz Okoro," a smartly dressed black woman said. "And this is Alice. She's Bernie's niece."

"And you're here to protest something?"

"The arrest of Niamh Devon."

"That arrest is not public knowledge," Walker said sternly.

"This is Invergryff," Alice said with a shrug. "You can't fart without half the town hearing about it."

"No need to be crude," Bernie said primly, while Walker tried to keep his face straight.

"Did I miss it?" A voice called out from behind a giant balloon that appeared to be Peppa Pig.

"Now that is definitely not a placard," Bernie said.

"Oh, it's for wee Frankie in primary one, I said to his mum I'd pick it up." The woman whose head was obscured by the giant pig hadn't realised that she'd let go of the string. Just at the last moment Walker leaned over and grabbed it.

"Careful now," he said, handing it over to the woman who he now realised was Mary Plunkett.

"Thanks," she said primly, tying the balloon around her wrist.

"Hello, Mrs Plunkett," Walker said, trying out his friendliest smile.

The woman gave him a solid glare. Just great.

"I think we might have gotten off on the wrong foot."

She crossed her arms, the action making Peppa's head bob to and fro in an alarming fashion. "Is that so?"

"I didn't mean to insult you," Walker said quickly. Actually, he wasn't even particularly sure what he'd done wrong, but he had always found with women that the bigger apology the better. "In fact, we value local input."

The woman's glare didn't soften. "Do you have sensitivity training, stuff like that?"

"More than you can possibly imagine," Walker replied.

"Well, you should probably pay more attention next time."

"Noted. Now can we stop arguing and discuss the case?"

She paused for a second. "You mean you are actually going to listen to me?"

He pulled her to one side, out of earshot of the world's smallest and angriest protest. "I think there's a chance that

Niamh Devon might not be the killer. You and your friends believe the same. Perhaps we could talk about it."

She stared at him for a moment, then inclined her head. "All right. If you come around tonight sometime after seven, we can chat. But only for five minutes, okay? If I put the kids to bed late they are like miniature ninjas the next day."

"Fine by me."

Chapter 46: Bernie

Bernie was feeling very pleased with the protest. They had gotten thirty-seven names on their petition to free Niamh Devon and the *Gazette* had even sent a photographer down to take some photos. They might even make the front page.

"You'll take Sean for a couple of hours then," Liz said, shoving the placards into the boot of her range rover. Bernie noticed it still had a dent all along the front bumper.

"Of course. I'll drop the kids at home and Finn will keep an eye on them," she said, knowing that that meant the kids would be plonked in front of the telly while Finn had a beer in the other room. Not that the kids would notice.

"Great. I'm off to get a peek at Niamh's laptop."

"And you're sure they will let you?"

"You're not the only one with contacts," Liz said with a smug smile. Bernie wanted to ask who, but she bit down on the question. It was so annoying when people tried to be enigmatic.

"You're popping into work then?" Liz asked.

"Yes. Not for a shift, just to see Annie."

"How is she?"

Bernie shrugged. "Not much better. I thought I might bring her some flowers. There's that place near the hospital that does nice ones."

"They've shut down. But there's a new spot opened up near the fishmongers. A bit expensive, and a few too many diamantes for my liking, but the bouquets are nice."

"Perfect. Come on kids, let's get home."

Sean and Ewan chattered happily all the way home, in the way that precocious only children often did. Bernie sorted them out some snacks and with a quick peck on the cheek for Finn she was on her way to the care home.

Bernie grabbed a bouquet of tulips from the flower shop that Liz had mentioned – cheaper than roses, plus no annoying thorns – and drove to the home.

As she arrived at Annie McGillivray's door, she took a moment before knocking. For the first time this week, she had stopped thinking about the murder case. Lucy had texted this morning to say that Annie wasn't eating, and was 'not good'. Well, there wasn't any need for more than that to be said when you worked in a care home. Just what would be on the other side of the door? Bernie raised her fist and knocked loudly.

"Come in," Anne said and Bernie let breathed out a sigh of relief.

The figure in the armchair was skinnier than ever, but still there. Still Annie McGillivray for a little while longer at least.

"Ah, it's yourself. Come and sit down. Are those for me?"

"Yes."

"I love yellow flowers. Always so cheerful. If you'd brought lilies I'd have tanned your backside you know."

"I know." Bernie found a vase on one of the bookshelves and popped the tulips into it.

"I've been hearing all about your adventures."

"From who?" Bernie asked.

"From your niece. The one with the pretty face and the peculiarly dyed hair."

"That would be Alice. I didn't realise you had even met her."

"Remember when I offered you the house? It was about a year ago, when you started your club. You got Alice to drop around a bottle of rum to say thank you."

"We owe you more than a bottle of rum," Bernie said. It was a sore point that Annie would never take any of the profits from the WWC, despite the fact that she kept offering her rent for the house.

"What would I do with any more money? Especially now. That Doctor with the extraordinary beard came in today. I asked him if he was a Sikh, but he said he just liked the style. Can you imagine? I'm sure it's not hygienic, but it does look very fine. Anyway, he said that it won't be long. That I should 'get my affairs in order'. I told him that I'd already let Pat Cash and John McEnroe down gently."

Bernie snorted back a laugh. "You've got a thing for tennis players?"

"Always had. Don't suppose you can arrange me a young Wimbledon wildcard for my final week on this earth?"

How easy it was to slip from laughter to tears, but Bernie was determined to hold them back for now.

"Even I can't work miracles, Annie. So what exactly has Alice been telling you?"

"That the dead body was that feckless young teacher, Mr Jones. I don't know, in my day people thought of teaching as a calling. It's not like it's well paid: why bother if you're not suited to it? Mind you, from what I've been hearing about poor Sam Jones he might not have been well suited to any sort of work. So many young men are like that."

"What have you been hearing about Sam Jones?"

"Well, it's been the talk of the home, of course. Vera Macbeth, you know, the one with sciatica all down her right leg, she was convinced that he had been 'offed by the mob'. I said to her what's the mob going to do in Invergryff? Start a protection racket with Crystal's Greengrocers and that Newsagents on Spencer Street that only opens on Saturdays? Please."

"Any more useful information?"

"A few things. I made some notes on the paper next to the crossword. Would you pass it over here?"

Bernie pretended not to notice how much the woman's hands were shaking when she held up the paper.

"Well, I tried calling some of my teacher friends, but do you know every one of them has retired now? Some days I feel older than others. Anyway, one of my probationers who just retired knew someone who knew someone and I ended up talking to Sam Jones's old HT down in England somewhere. What was her name? Oh yes, Mrs Newton. Nice lady, Welsh accent."

Bernie leaned forward. "What did Mrs Newton have to say?"

"Well, she was pretty careful at first, but when she heard I was head myself for twenty years, she loosened up. Turns out that when your Mr Jones was in school there were some problems with the petty cash. And some not so petty cash as well. Jones had volunteered to help out with some of the financial admin and the figures never quite added up. Never got to the point of actual allegations, but right before it did, he resigned. Off he went to Scotland, and I got the feeling Mrs Newton felt that it was good riddance and no mistake."

"That is interesting," Bernie said. "Anything else."

Annie rubbed at her chest.

"Are you cold? Can I get you anything?"

"Don't you start mothering me now, Bernadette Paterson. I still remember when you couldn't do your six times table."

"Sorry."

"The only other thing of interest was that Mrs Hall in room twenty-one thinks that he went out with that girl from the shoe shop that always gets the sizes wrong. Apparently, she was fair upset when he ditched her. Sent her sister round to shout at him and all."

"It's Sharon that works in the shoe shop. We've spoken to her already. She has an alibi."

"Those things are always fake on the telly."

"True," Bernie said. "I'll double-check." It was raining hard now, big splattering drops making their way down the window.

"Well, you better be off then. That murder won't solve itself." Annie sat up straight in the chair and when Bernie hugged her there was nothing more than a skeleton under her dress.

"See you soon, Annie."

"Don't bet on it, Bernie."

Chapter 47: Mary

When Mary arrived back home she let the older kids run upstairs and gave her mother a hug.

"How was Lauren?"

"Wee angel as ever. She's napping upstairs right now."

Great, Mary thought, that means she'll barely sleep tonight.

"I've left you a box of dairy milk in the cupboard. Ellis from next door gave it to me for giving him some cuttings of a hydrangea, but I'm off lactose at the moment."

"Thanks mum," Mary said, giving her another squeeze. "It's you that's the angel."

"Don't be silly. I'm off home now, you all right to take over?"

No mum, Mary thought. My marriage is a wreck and I'm broke and I have no idea what I'm going to do.

"Of course."

Her mum disappeared out of the door. Mary called up to the kids to tidy up, mainly so that she could have five minutes to herself.

The five minutes never happened. Before Mary had had time to grab a cup of tea, the kids had all ran downstairs and started turning the living room into an obstacle course. This had woken Lauren up, who had tried to join in but somehow ended up being sick behind a cushion. Two seconds later Peter had slipped over trying to use the books for a game of floor is lava and Mary had spilled the cup of tea all over her favourite slippers.

"What else could go wrong?" Vikki asked as she handed her mother the all-purpose upholstery cleaner. Lauren was sitting watching cartoons as if nothing had happened.

Mary narrowed her eyes. "Probably not a good idea to say that. Don't you think it's tempting fate a little?"

"I don't believe in fate. Just like Gods and the tooth fairy."

"All right, all right. Keep your voice down. Maybe we could just –"

"Mum! The sink's blocked!"

Mary just had enough time to mutter the word 'see!' to her daughter as she raced into the kitchen. Peter was standing next to the offending sink which was making an ominous gurgling noise.

"Turn off the tap! What did you do to it?"

"Nothing!"

"Are you sure?" The trouble was, Peter's face always looked perfectly innocent. Like a cherub, if that cherub was using its magic arrows to poke one of its siblings in the eye.

"Sure, mum." His eyes were filling with actual tears of indignation.

"Right. Well. I suppose I'll have to take a look at it."

"Shouldn't we get a plumber?" Vikki Little Miss Sensible asked.

Call out charges, Mary thought. Not to mention whatever it would cost to fix the blooming thing.

"Why don't you take Johnny and Peter outside for a jump on the trampoline while I take a look at it," she said.

"Okay," Vikki replied, then spent five minutes shouting at her brothers until they were all safely out in the garden. With Lauren having a post-vomit rest on the sofa, Mary had a moment of silence before her own sigh broke it.

"Let's have a look at this sink then." She pulled on her pink marigolds and grabbed the screwdriver from the cutlery drawer that was the extent of her tool collection. She propped her phone up in front of her, playing videos on how to dismantle a kitchen sink. It looked easy enough.

Ten sweaty minutes later, Mary was using a towel to try and get enough purchase to remove the plastic grey pipe that seemed to be causing all the problems.

"Right, off you come!" she yelled as she pulled with all her might.

What Mary hadn't realised was that the sink trap would also come loose. The pressure of the water forced it out of its connection and caused everything inside to come shooting out at full speed, right into her face.

"Ugh!" Black slime coated everything between her eyebrows and her stomach. "What the f—"

"Are you okay mummy?" Johnny asked, sticking his head in the back door with perfect timing.

"I'm fine, sweetheart. Just having a little… difficult moment. No, don't come in!" I'm a private investigator, Mary thought, just like Poirot. How come he never had to deal with this crap?

"Wow! How did you make the sink explode? That is so awesome!" Johnny shouted, dancing around the kitchen in excitement.

There was something strange about her child, but the sludge dripping off her chin was making it hard to think.

"Johnny, where are your trousers?"

"I buried them in the garden."

"Of course you did. Now you get back outside and –"

Just at that moment the doorbell rang.

"Oh bloody hell!"

"I'll get it mum," Johnny said, skipping over to the door.

"Wait! You've got no trousers on!" Dripping wet, Mary pulled her head out from under the sink and scurried after her half-naked son. She reached the front door just as he yanked it open.

"Hello young man."

Mary scraped the gunk from her eyes so that she could see who it was.

"Oh. Nice to see you again, Constable. Aren't you a bit early?"

"I was at a loose end so I thought I'd see if you were free. You have a little… substance on you."

Mary looked down at her muck-splattered torso. "I am having some minor plumbing issues," she said.

"The sink exploded!" Johnny yelled happily.

"And did it blow your trousers off too?"

"No! I buried them in the garden."

"Oh." Walker seemed lost for words.

Mary managed to pull herself together. "It's not a good time. The sink is pouring water as we speak. Do you need to ask me something important? Or maybe you've come to arrest Johnny for indecent exposure?"

"Can I go to jail?" Johnny hopped from one foot to the other. "That would be cool."

Walker laughed. "How about I ask your mum some questions while I take a look at the sink? My dad was a plumber, so I'm pretty handy."

"I bet you are," Mary said, then instantly blushed. "I mean, I'll just go and grab a change for Johnny, then I'll meet you in the kitchen."

"Great," Walker said, taking off his coat and rolling up his shirt sleeves. I must not fancy him, Mary said to herself. It is very important not to consider his muscly arms. He is the enemy.

"Mum? Trousers?"

"Yes, of course. Come on upstairs and we'll get you sorted."

Chapter 48: Mary

While Johnny was putting some trousers on, Mary took the opportunity to change her own top and wash the worst of the slime from her face. From downstairs there was a combination of manly grunting, hammering on pipes and, worryingly, the odd childish giggle.

"Why don't you let the Constable work in peace," Mary said when she walked into the kitchen to see the audience of delighted faces surrounding poor Walker who was folded up under the sink in a position that did not look comfortable. Even Lauren had made a miraculous recovery to gawp at the policeman.

"Thanks," he said once the children disappeared. "Um. Your oldest son…"

"That would be Peter."

"I think he nicked my handcuffs."

Five minutes and some raised voices later, the handcuffs were replaced and the sink appeared to be fixed.

"What was wrong with it?"

Walker held up a muck-covered plastic item about the size of his fist. "I think it had a case of the stegosauruses."

Mary closed her eyes. "Is it illegal to batter your own children?"

"Afraid so."

"Thanks for helping with the sink. And, um, I'm very sorry about your shirt."

Constable Walker's normal scent of citrus aftershave had been replaced by the distinct tang of sink goop and there were trails of grime all over his regulation police clothing.

"Can I make you a tea?"

Walker's mouth turned down at the corners. "How about we just have a chat."

"Let's go into the living room. We might actually get some peace there."

Hoping that he wouldn't notice the vomit smell that was still lurking under half a can of floral air freshener, Mary led the Constable over to the sofa.

"I don't suppose you've released Niamh Devon yet," Mary said.

"No. And even though I still have questions, the evidence is compelling. I was hoping you might share with me anything that you've managed to come up with. We need another suspect if we're going to cast doubt on Niamh Devon being the killer."

"I guess we're a bit low on suspects too."

Walker rubbed at his forehead. "Thing is, we still haven't worked out how he met half of these women. We know that he didn't like dating locals."

"Online dating, wasn't it?"

"Not that we can see. Nothing on his phone."

"I'm sure Sharon said that was how they met," Mary said.

There was a sudden pause in the conversation.

"Do you mean Sharon Macdonald?

"Sharon from the shoe shop," Mary said. "I don't think I ever knew her last name."

Walker checked his tablet. "That's right, she works in a shoe shop. My colleague interviewed her."

"And so did I. Is there a problem with that?"

Walker sighed. "I'm not happy about it, but as you've made perfectly clear, I can't stop you from speaking to these people. But if you interfere in the case…"

"I know, I know. Do not pass go, straight to jail. Do you want to know about Sharon Macdonald or not?"

Walker folded his arms. "Sure."

"She went out with Sam Jones, but they split up two years ago. And I'm sure she said they met online. Hang on, let me check." She rooted around in her pocket for her notepad. "Yes, here it is. His username was Sexysam87. Talk about a red flag."

"Thanks," Walker said, keying the name into his tablet. "I don't suppose you know what the app was."

"No, sorry. Either she didn't mention it or I've forgotten. When I was last single these things barely existed." Christ, Mary thought, how long before she would have to join one of these websites. Sexymumoffour84? It didn't bear thinking about.

"No matter, we'll work it out."

"You know, I couldn't help but feel that Sharon was a bit more cut up about Sam Jones dumping her than she was making out."

Walker checked the tablet again. "Looks like she had an alibi for Thursday night."

"So she said."

"We do check these things, you know."

"I know," Mary said, although privately she decided that she would double-check it herself. The police might be good at fixing sinks, but they didn't seem to be very good at catching Sam Jones's murderer.

"Anything else that might help?"

"We've a few things in the pipeline," Mary said vaguely. "Maybe I could let you know when we find something."

"Here's my number. Um, my personal one, just in case you can't get through to me at the station."

Was he blushing a little as he said it? Mary put the number into her phone.

There was the thudding of feet running in from outside.

"It's raining, mum!"

"All right," Mary said, shoeing them upstairs. "Take your shoes off and —"

"There's someone in your back garden!" Walker shouted, running past her towards the back door.

"What?"

"They just climbed over the fence!" The police officer shouted something else unintelligible and rushed out into the garden.

There was someone all right, a man in jeans and a black hoodie who was heading for the house. In an instant Walker tackled him, bringing him down onto the ground.

"Aah!" The man screamed as Walker forced his hand behind his back."

"Don't worry, I've got him," Walker said, just as Mary caught a glimpse of a red face covered in dirt.

"Oh god, let him go!" Mary said, her hands to her face. "That's my husband!"

Chapter 49: Liz

The Nigerian community in Invergryff was something like the mafia in 1930's New York, only with better dress sense. This was in spite of the fact that it was made up of less than a dozen families. Liz's mum and dad had been two of the first to come over from Africa, and that gave them a certain kudos in the community. Liz herself had always been a little frightened of the Aunties and Uncles that invaded her parents' house every weekend. They always seemed to know exactly what you had been up to, and were never shy of telling you what they thought about it. At least it had provided her with a contact to get her into Invergryff Primary School.

"I thought you were a big shot accountant," Fiona Omoregie said, one hand on her hip. "Why are you wanting to check out the IT at the school?"

"Well, that's a bit of a long story," Liz said, shuffling from one foot to the other while she figured out what to say. Fiona was eight years younger than her, but Liz had always found her kind of intimidating. She had a nose stud and hair that was shaved on one side. She looked like she should have been in an edgy music video, not in a school IT department.

"Is it about the kids' internet profiles? We sent a message about it last week. Honestly, it's nothing to worry about."

"Yes, that's it," Liz replied, seizing on the opportunity. "I've been hearing from Sean that they've been on some slightly dodgy websites and I wanted to check it out."

Fiona sniffed. "We have a very prohibitive firewall setup here."

"Oh, I'm sure it's nothing that could be laid at your feet," Liz said with a bright smile. "I just wondered if you could show me how it all works."

"I suppose I could. Why don't you come along to my office?"

Fiona's office was small, with just two desks and, disconcertingly, a poster of Scott and Charlene from *Neighbours* on the wall.

"Big fan of Kylie are you?" Liz asked, pointing at the poster.

"Not exactly. It's kind of ironic."

Feeling totally lost, Liz sat down opposite Fiona and watched as she navigated the school's computer files. Just as Fiona got to the point where she was accessing internet profiles, Liz started to cough.

Just a little at first, then a sort of choked bark.

"Liz?"

"I just need a second. Frog in my throat." Liz coughed some more.

"Are you okay?"

"Could you get me a glass of water?" Liz wheezed. "I just need something to drink."

"Of course!" Fiona ran out of the office. Liz waited a second then shut the door behind her. She sat down in front of the screen and scanned the files as quickly as she could. Luckily in her line of work you had to know your way around a computer.

It took less than a minute for her to locate Niamh Devon's profile. Liz went into her documents folder and quickly scrolled through. It all looked annoyingly professional, and there were no photos at all. She slipped the memory drive she had brought with her and copied it all across anyway. There was no sound of Fiona returning, so she clicked back through the folders until she found the one for Sam Jones. She copied that all across as well.

One minute for file transfer.

Liz tapped her nails on the desk. The seconds ticked down. Then the sound of footsteps came from the corridor.

Transfer complete.

Liz pulled the memory drive out of the computer and tucked it into her jeans pocket just as Fiona pulled the door open.

"I've got your water," she said, panting, then frowned when she saw where Liz was sitting.

"Hang on," Fiona said, coming around to the other side of the desk. "That's not the kids' profiles. That's the section for the staff."

"Is it?" Liz said, trying to look innocent. "Sorry, I just thought I'd speed things up a little. I was looking for the internet history but I got a little lost."

"What the hell are you playing at?" Fiona looked seriously annoyed. "I'm going to call the Head."

"No! Please don't, I'm just checking out something on Niamh Devon's account. You know that the police have arrested her. It might get her out of jail."

"Oh holy hell, you're not allowed to do that! I'm going to have to tell Mrs Figgis what you've been up to."

"Please, Fiona, I –"

"I'm calling her right now."

"I wouldn't do that," Liz said, leaning across the desk. "Not unless you want Auntie Abeke to know what really happened to Uncle Mo's Ford Fiesta on Christmas Eve in 1998."

"You wouldn't dare!" Fiona said, her bottom lip trembling. Liz knew she had her.

"Just try me. Look, I'm not trying to cause trouble. I'm actually trying to help out one of your colleagues."

Fiona got up and opened the door. "I never liked Niamh anyway. She was always creeping about after that Sam Jones. Wouldn't surprise me one bit if she killed him."

"Well, if that's the case I'll find out too. Thanks Fiona."

"Don't come back." The office door slammed shut behind her.

When Liz got back to her car she sent Bernie a message.

Got kicked out of the school. Will call later.

Just as she put the key in the ignition her phone buzzed. Liz picked it up, expecting to see a reply from Bernie, but it was Amy from work calling. She probably shouldn't answer, Liz thought, even though her finger was already over the green button.

"Hello?"

"I've been trying to message you. It's all going nuts at work. Didn't Phil call?"

"I don't think so," Liz said, not wanting to say that she had blocked his number.

"Well you need to get over here. The bosses are all shouting at each other. They've found more discrepancies in the accounts. It's all kicking off and it looks like they're going to pin it on you."

"On me?"

"Look, I need to go. I'm pretending to have a pee just to call you. Honestly, Liz, you need to get over here right away."

"I'm coming," Liz said, all thoughts of murder forgotten. "I just need to get my bag."

Chapter 50: Liz

What the hell was going on at work? Liz drove back to her house as fast as she could without getting pulled over. When she got there she had a quick glance at her blocked numbers. Sure enough, Phil had been trying to phone. Dammit, how was she meant to know that it would be something serious?

She hurried into the house and grabbed her laptop. She paused for a second then rooted into her drawers and took out the speech recorder that she and Bernie had bought for the WWC. If the poop was going to hit the fan, Liz wanted to at least have evidence of what was happening.

She pulled the front door open, ready to run to the car, and instead walked straight into Bernie.

"Going somewhere?" Bernie asked.

"Big work drama," Liz said, pushing past her friend and locking the front door. "I can't talk now."

"But you need to tell me what happened at the school. Why did they kick you out?"

"Not now for God's sake." Liz dropped her bag in a hurry to get the car keys. She grabbed it and hurried around to the driver's side. Bernie was blocking the car door, standing in front of it with her arms crossed.

"What is this, some sort of intervention?" Liz asked, only half joking. She didn't like the fierce expression on her friend's face.

"Sort of," Bernie said. "I need to talk to you."

"I need to get to work."

"Not right now you don't."

"Bernie, we've been friends for years, but I'm telling you that you are walking on thin ice right now."

"You made a commitment to me, Liz. I thought we both wanted this WWC thing to work."

"We do!"

"Then what's all this work crap?"

"I don't know. There's some sort of emergency –"

"Come off it. You get text messages every day, even after work hours. I think it's about time you tell me what's going on with your phone. Are you having an affair?"

"What? God, no."

"You know I wouldn't judge you if you were."

Liz laughed. "Yes you would! But, honestly, I'm not having an affair. It's just work."

"No work messages you every hour, even on the weekend."

"Mine does."

"Then you need to tell them to stop! It's not right, being constantly on edge like that. I can see how tense you are. And

I need you to focus on our murder case."

"Look, it really is a work emergency."

Bernie didn't move. Liz wondered if she was actually going to have to push her out of the way.

"Tell me," Bernie said.

"Okay," Liz said, hearing the buzz of more text messages arriving on her phone through the fabric of her pocket. "There has been a thing with one of the guys at work. Phil. He's been texting me all the time ever since we had a falling out last year. But there's no affair or anything."

"Sounds like he wants one."

"No. It's just…" Liz rubbed her eyes. She was sick of lying about everything. "The thing is, Phil covered up a mistake I made. Sorted it all out for me. It was a pretty bad thing, a sackable offence, in fact. And I thought he was being a good guy by taking the fall. Of course, now he's been holding it over my head ever since. It's been a bloody nightmare."

"Jesus, Liz, that's harassment. You need to report the guy!"

"Because it's always that simple?" Liz bit back. "It might be for you. Not for me."

"What does that mean?"

"It means he's already accused me of 'playing the race card'. If he puts it around that I'm making complaints just because I'm black and he's white, well, that sort of rumour will kill my career."

"I'm guessing it's your gender that's the problem for him, not your race."

Liz shrugged. "It's both, of course."

"Then that's precisely why you can't let him get away with it!"

"You have no idea what you're talking about, Bernie," Liz snapped.

"Come on now, just sit down and let's talk about this," Bernie said.

"No thank you. Just because you want to talk about something, doesn't mean I want to. I'm going to go to work."

Finally Bernie took the hint and moved out of the way. She didn't say a word while Liz started up the car and drove off. The last thing Liz saw was Bernie's face, pinched and angry, as she pulled out of the drive.

Chapter 51: Mary

Mary helped Walker get Matt up from the ground. He had mud all over his cheek where the Constable had pushed him into the mud, but apart from that, he looked the same as ever.

"What the hell, Mary, did you call the cops on me?"

"No! This is Constable Walker, he was just helping with the sink."

"What?" Matt shook his head, like he was dazed. "Is he a policeman or a plumber?"

"Police officer," Walker said, and Mary noticed his face was flushed with embarrassment. "I'm sorry for the confusion, Mr Plunkett. May I ask why you were climbing over the fence?"

"I thought I would surprise the kids if they were playing out back." Matt said.

"Seems an odd choice when you could have rang the doorbell," Walker said.

"You nearly broke my leg," Matt said, getting more indignant now he was over his initial shock.

Mary rubbed her temples. "Listen Matt, just go upstairs and see the kids."

"All right," her husband said, giving Walker another dark look as he left.

"And think about your excuse for turning up here without warning," Mary hissed as he walked past. "And it better be a good one or I'll break your leg for real this time."

Walker was left standing awkwardly in the garden.

"Sorry about that," Mary said. "I had no idea he was going to turn up today."

"I know. It's just… man, what if I had broken his leg? He could have pressed charges. I mean, he could still…"

"I'll talk to him," Mary said. She had never seen Walker look worried before. "I'll explain what happened. Matt won't want to cause a fuss. Believe me."

"I thought you were in trouble. Messing about in the investigation, then I see someone breaking in… I shouldn't have come here in the first place."

"Look, Matt's my husband, but we are separated. He lives in Aberdeen. There was no way I could have known he was going to turn up." Mary looked down at her feet.

"So he's here without permission? Has he been threatening you?"

Mary realised that if she said so she could have the stupid bugger taken away in handcuffs. But he was still the kids' father, wasn't he? And he was still *something* to her, even if she wasn't quite sure what that was.

"No. He's just your ordinary idiot ex. I'm sorry, Walker, but it's not a police matter at all. I'm fine, honestly."

"Right. I misinterpreted the situation. I'll head back to the station."

Mary just opened the door for him. What else was there to do? She tried not to see the hurt expression on his face as he left.

Chapter 52: Mary

Upstairs were sounds of sheer delight as the children realised that their father was in the house. Mary had poured herself a very strong cup of tea and was trying to think what to do. She was determined not to wonder what the handsome police officer had thought about the whole debacle in the back garden. Just as he was starting to think of her as a proper investigator, now he would think she was a flaky, married idiot. Which she was, of course.

The tea was so strong that it coated her tongue. Never mind Constable Walker, what exactly was she going to do about Matt? She could hardly kick him out this second, like she wanted to. The kids would be devastated. So as usual she had to just suck it up.

"Did you put the kettle on?" Matt asked, popping his head around the door.

"You can make yourself a tea if you want one."

Matt did just that, fishing a teabag out of the packet. "Lauren's hair is so long."

"I know. I have to brush it every morning."

"Bet she loves that."

Mary laughed. "Yeah, she squeals like a piglet. Vikki does it for her sometimes. Saves me time in the mornings."

"If you were back home, I could help."

She had known that the conversation was coming, but that didn't make it any easier. "This is home now, Matt. We won't be coming back to Aberdeen."

Matt sniffed in a way that reminded her so much of Peter she almost cried there and then. "I don't suppose that policeman has anything to do with it?"

Mary shrugged. "What, you think I've got time for a boyfriend?"

"He looked like he had his feet under the table."

"Don't be stupid. Actually, he was here to ask me about a case."

"Really? You mean you were serious about all that private investigator stuff? I thought you were making it up."

"Why would I do that?"

"Well, you've always been a fan of madcap ideas. Remember when you decided to make crochet blankets as a side hustle? Or when you started baking cakes for other people? Lewis from the bank still talks about the time you made his son a coffin cake."

"It was meant to be a piano. Anyway, this is different. Besides, I need the money"

Matt scratched at a patch of skin behind his ear. "You know that I'm working on that, right? I've been going to meetings."

"Every week?"

He shrugged. "Most."

"And you've stayed off the websites?"

"Cross my heart," he said, smiling at her.

"It's not a joke, Matt. You are a gambling addict. You need to get it sorted."

"And then you'll come back?"

Mary shook her head. "You know that's not going to happen. But at least you'll have a decent relationship with your kids. You've still got a chance to fix that one."

"It's just... Look, I know I screwed up. I've got an addiction. But it's not like I slept with someone else."

"I honestly think that might have been better," Mary said.

"You don't mean that. Come on, Mary, it's only money at the end of the day."

How did he always manage to make her the bad guy? "It's not just money though, is it? It's a betrayal. The thing is, yes, I was angry when I found out that you stole from me. When I found out that you'd mortgaged our lovely house up to the hilt. But I could have found a way to forgive you then."

"You still can!"

"Maybe I could have. But then I checked the kids' savings accounts. And do you know what I found? You'd taken every penny, hadn't you? Lauren got twenty quid in a cheque from her gran one day, and you'd removed it an hour later. You stole from our babies, Matt. I can't ever forgive you for that."

Chapter 53: Walker

When Constable Walker had left Mary Plunkett's house, he had been furious with the woman and her not-so-ex-husband. By the time he had driven away in the squad car he was mainly annoyed with himself. What exactly had he been playing at? He was attracted to her, and that was incredibly stupid. Did he think that she would swoon all over him just because he fixed her sink? Why would she, when she had a husband to do it anyway?

At least she had told him something useful. Despite the police finding no evidence of the fact, Sam Jones had used dating apps. Walker needed to take another look at the teacher's phone.

He grabbed a pre-packed sandwich from a supermarket on the way to the station – his third of the week, not a good sign – and hurried into the office.

"Let me guess, you've cracked the case?" Neil said, looking up from his phone.

"Not yet."

"Still don't think it's Niamh Devon?"

Walker shrugged. "There's enough doubt there to look at other people. Jury might think so too."

"It was your evidence that led to her arrest, remember," Neil said.

"I know, and there was definitely sufficient grounds. It's just that when you get right down to it, I can't imagine her murdering him. Not in such a cold-blooded way."

"Didn't they teach you at police college that murderers rarely look like murderers?" Neil chuckled.

"Have you got Jones's phone handy?" Walker said, not wanting to waste any more time.

"Sure. I think it's on Macleod's desk. He's off to see the Superintendent about something."

Walker looked through the evidence bags on the Inspector's desk and found the phone. Neil arrived beside him.

"We've looked at everything on that, you know. Clean as a whistle."

"You remember the ex-girlfriend, Sharon somebody?"

"Sure. Works in a shoe shop and smokes like a chimney."

"That's the one. Well, she says that Jones got in touch with her on a dating app."

Neil frowned. "We didn't find any dating apps on his phone."

"I know. That's why I thought I'd take another look."

He turned the phone on and scrolled through the apps. There were the usual things, streaming apps, a couple of games, the standard social media sites that Walker knew the techs had already taken a good look at.

"There's a folder here called teaching resources," Walker said, pointing at the icon. "Do you think they checked here?"

He went into the folder and there were three apps. One was for Maths, one for Science and one for French.

"Seems legit," Neil said.

Walker's hope was fading fast. Desperate, he clicked on the icon for Maths, which was an old-fashioned abacus.

Welcome back to Single and Successful.

"That's it!" Walker shouted. "A dating app."

"Hey, he changed the icon somehow," Neil said, leaning over the phone. "Made it look like a school thing. Why would he do that?"

"So that he could check his dating profile at work, I imagine," Walker said, already navigating through the menu to find the messages section.

"Sly dog," Neil added. "Let's have a look at what he's been up to."

Walker clicked on recent messages.

"Jesus, there's hundreds of them," Neil said. "Put it up on the smartboard will you?"

After struggling with the cables for a moment, Walker worked out how to put the phone's display on the screen.

"Macleod's going to be pissed we missed these," Neil said.

"Yeah," Walker replied. "Let's see if we can find anything that might cheer him up."

It took them an hour to go through all the messages from the last year. Sam Jones had liked to spread his net wide. He was in contact with forty women, although many of the conversations had only been a couple of messages before one person (generally the woman) lost interest and stopped replying.

"I hear you've got something on the phone," Macleod said, dumping a box of files on the table. It was amazing how much paperwork was generated in the paperless office.

Neil stepped forward. For a moment, Walker thought he was going to take all the credit and he felt his back stiffen.

"The Constable worked it out, Rob. The dating apps were hidden behind some icons that looked like teaching stuff. We should have spotted it earlier."

"Yes, you bloody well should have," Macleod barked. "But so should I, so we'll let it drop, shall we? Well done, Walker, let's see what you've found."

Glowing inside from Macleod's praise, Walker stepped in front of the smartboard to explain what was being displayed.

"There were hundreds of messages from three different apps," Walker explained. "We went back over the last three years to find them all. To narrow it down, we've eliminated any women that didn't reply back. Which was nearly fifty, by the way."

"Jones was a determined guy," Neil added.

"Might have been better for the lad if he'd found a different hobby," Macleod said. "So once you get rid of the rejects, who is left?"

"About thirty that he actually had a conversation with. Maybe half of them he met up with. I'm checking through them, but it's tricky. They don't always use their real names on the site."

"Damn," Macleod said. "That's too many."

"I know. There's a couple we can rule out though. I've already found Sharon from the shoe shop, and Cheryl, the one that came into the station to say that she'd seen him in the pub that night. Apart from them, I think we've got half a dozen women that might fit our profile."

"What about the most recent messages?"

Walker nodded. "That's where it gets interesting. He had a few women he was messaging in the week leading up to his death."

"First we've got LadyG who appears about six months ago. Photos show a blond around the right age. Not anyone we've interviewed already. They send a few messages, then Jones mentions meeting up eight weeks ago and she gives him her number. There doesn't seem to be any messages on his phone from her number, so either LadyG ditched him, or he deleted them."

"Interesting. Can you follow that up?"

"Will do. But there's one more that might be our woman. A username of Scotchick85, she appears on the app only last month. Her profile pictures are all in soft focus or silhouette, so it's impossible to tell what she looks like."

"Let me guess, that didn't stop Jones?"

"He certainly seemed to have a wide spectrum of taste. He starts messaging her two weeks ago, and then the messages stop just two days before he dies."

"Is there a chance that this Scotchick85 is the same as the unknown mobile number that messaged him about meeting up?"

"A good chance, I'd say. If we could see her phone we could prove it."

"We'll need to find her first. Take another look through her profile and see if you can come up with the name. Neil, you get on to the owners of the dating app. Of course, they'll probably winge about data protection or something, but see if you can twist their arm and give us some names."

"All right."

"Well, you know what you've got to do. And remember, if we don't find any other viable suspects, we'll be charging Niamh Devon within the hour, so let's get it right."

Chapter 54: Liz

Liz wished she had had time to change her shoes. The black boots had very high heels which meant that she was in danger of twisting an ankle as she speed-walked along the corridor. She had to try very hard to resist the urge to run. If what she thought was happening was happening, then it was important that she made a good first impression. Limping into the room full of directors, sweaty and panting, would not be a wise choice.

As she sped through the building, she rang Amy, "I'm here," she hissed. "What's going on?"

"Thanks, mum," Amy said in a nervous voice. "I'm in a meeting right now. I'll call you later, okay. I've left your lunch on the table. You know, where you usually sit."

The call clicked off.

"Damn!" Liz said. She had reached her office. There didn't seem to be anyone else left on this floor. This did not feel like a good sign. She went over to her desk, and sure enough, there was a file there. Amy had left a post-it on top that just said 'urgent'. Well, that was clear enough.

There simply wasn't enough time for Liz to look through all the paperwork, so she scanned as much as she could. Something was seriously wrong with these files. Maybe she should –

"Liz?"

Mr Oliver stood in the doorway, and he didn't look very happy.

"Yes?" Liz tucked the file into her bag before he noticed it.

"We've been trying to get in touch with you. There's an emergency meeting of senior staff going on upstairs right now."

"I just got the message, Mr Oliver. I wanted to grab my things before heading upstairs."

"You can walk with me."

Was Liz being paranoid, or did he not want her walking around the office alone? She followed him up the stairs, enjoying the fact that Mr Oliver was out of breath a lot quicker than she was.

When her boss opened the door to the meeting room, Liz was glad she had been warned about what to expect. All the senior members of the Invergryff office were there, along with Joan Peters, the head of personnel and Ben Forbes, the head of pretty much everything from the company headquarters in Glasgow.

"Sit down please, Liz," Ben Forbes said. No one as much as met her eyes, apart from Amy who gave her a grim smile. Liz took her seat and tried to relax her shoulders. If she was going to go down she was going to do it calmly, without giving them the satisfaction of seeing her emotions.

"We've just been summarizing what we've learned over the last twenty-four hours. Phil, maybe you could recap for us."

"Sure," Phil said. He didn't seem nervous at all. If anything, he just looked shinier than normal. "I guess it was Ollie who flagged up the problems first. We were looking at the Bloom file and he noticed that the numbers didn't match across different documents. In the master document they looked fine, but the local one was not consistent. It looked like certain sums of money were unaccounted for."

"I must add that at this point we are not making any accusations," Joan Peters said, with a brittle grin. "Just trying to establish the facts."

Liz glanced around the room, but no one seemed to be looking at her. Was that because they thought she was guilty of something? Or because they were worried about their own jobs. Ben Forbes looked bored, checking his phone under the table. This was all small fry to him, Liz guessed. Not to her though.

Sitting to her right, Amy looked terrible. She was biting one of her acrylic nails and one set of false eyelashes was crooked. Surely she didn't have anything to worry about? Liz had always thought that Amy had cared more about having brunch with her pals than career ambitions. Could the girl have been dumb enough to risk it all for a bit of petty cash?

"We worked out that across several accounts a seven figure sum has gone missing in the last year."

"Sorry," Liz said, leaning forward over the cheap laminate table. "Did you say seven figures?"

"Yes," Ben Forbes said, looking up from his phone. "Someone has made a very expensive mistake. Or…"

"Or someone has stolen the money," Phil said.

"Again, we have no proof of that at this stage," Miss Peters reminded him with a scowl. "We're not making any accusations."

"Can you show me what you found?" Liz asked.

"Sure," Phil replied, giving her another smug smile. He's the one, Liz thought in a flash of inspiration. He had to be the one that stole the money. No one else would have the sheer arrogance to do it. But how did he think he was going to get away with it?

"It took me most of the last two days to figure it out," Phil said. "I would have contacted you, Liz, but I knew that you were busy."

Liz nodded, not trusting herself to reply to that one.

"Finally this morning it all clicked together. Since then, I've been sorting out the accounts. It looks like a lot of the money was returned, although there are still some smaller sums that I haven't been able to find. I've sorted out most of the company accounts before they noticed, at least."

Mr Oliver clapped his hand on Phil's back. "If it wasn't for Phil fighting fires for us all day, I don't know what we would have done without him. It's the company's reputation that's on the line."

Good old Phil. Liz was trying her best not to let her anger show on her face, but she wasn't sure she was pulling it off.

"Where to start?" Phil hooked his thumbs into his belt, like a wild west Sheriff. "The first incident occurred before Christmas last year. It involved the Home Energy account. Do you remember it?"

Oh crap. Liz couldn't help but stare at Phil. This was it, her big mistake. It looked like Phil had finally decided to rat her out.

"Fifty grand 'misplaced' from the account, then returned three days later. And someone had deleted the older files so that I had to go to the system back-up to work out what had happened. Clear evidence that there was a cover-up going on."

Liz clenched her fists under the table. She could feel her nails digging into her palms.

"It'll take a little time to go through the files, but it seems like all the trouble started in December last year. We had several new staff members join us around that time."

There was a gasp from Liz's right.

"Miss White, you joined the company in the December, didn't you?" Forbes asked, although he already knew the answer.

"You don't mean..." Amy's bottom lip wobbled.

"Let Phil finish, then we can see what's what," the HR woman said, and Liz noted she had stopped complaining about accusations.

Liz forced herself to smile. She had worked out how it was going to go down. Phil would blame Amy somehow, no doubt with clear 'evidence'. And all she had to do was keep quiet.

"Would you like to say anything, Liz?" Phil asked.

Liz bit her lip and looked down, giving him the slightest shake of the head. That was her choice then. Phil couldn't have spelled it out any more clearly. Either she kept quiet and let Amy go down for all of this. Or she stood up and confessed to her own mistake. Get fired immediately, of course, just to save Amy's job. It wasn't like the girl was even that good at it!

And if Liz owned up, got fired, what then? With that sort of black mark on her CV, she would struggle to get something else. How would she pay the mortgage? She had spent the last year lying for Phil, would one more little lie make any difference?

Chapter 56: Bernie

Some people dawdle when they walk down the street. Like they left the house and instantly forgot which way they were going. Mary Plunkett was definitely a dawdler. She probably stood still at the top of escalators too.

Bernie Paterson had never dawdled in her life. Even as a toddler, she was the one pulling her mother along by the reins, not the other way around. Or at least that was how she remembered it.

At the present moment, she was increasingly feeling like they were dawdling on the Sam Jones case. The police, incompetent as they were in general, had at least managed to arrest someone. Bernie was just as convinced as Liz was that Niamh was not the killer, but if nothing else it showed that the boys in blue weren't afraid of a little action. Where were the WWC's suspects?

Bernie had gone for a walk to clear her head. Plus, she knew that walking for an hour killed two hundred calories and she had definitely been neglecting her exercise recently. Just like when she was at the gym, she always felt like she did her best thinking when she was in motion. A woman in front of her had a pug that was choosing this moment to make its mark on the pavement. She turned and gave Bernie an 'isn't he sweet' look.

Bernie kept walking. In all honesty, she didn't understand pets. At least children grew up. If you had a puppy it was like having a baby that never got to the stage of learning how to use the toilet. Gross.

Sam Jones. Who killed him? Bernie pumped her legs faster. Mary Plunkett seemed to think that Sharon from the shoe shop was the one. The police thought it was Niamh Devon. Which was right? Bernie had no clue, and that was irritating her.

She checked her fitness watch and saw that she had been walking for an hour. Time to head home.

If you had asked Bernie to her face, she wouldn't have admitted that she was avoiding her husband, but it still took her a fraction of a second longer than it should have to open the front door.

"Nice walk?" Finn asked when she walked into the kitchen. There were three empty beer cans next to the sink. Was it better that he wasn't hiding them yet? Bernie reckoned it had to be.

"Okay. I was hoping I might have an epiphany or something?"

"Isn't she a French supermodel?"

Bernie couldn't help but laugh. "Shut it. I was hoping to find out who killed Sam Jones."

Finn shrugged. "I don't know why you're so bothered about it. It's not like it's any of your business."

Well, that was the thing. Bernie hadn't ever told her husband that it was her business. She had kept the money from the WWC in a separate savings account. Just in case. It was screwed up, but then what family wasn't?

"I guess I'm just interested. And I don't want Niamh Devon to go down for some crime that she didn't commit."

A thundering sound announced that two boys were coming down the stairs.

"Can we have a snack?" Ewan's round face appeared around the kitchen door, quickly followed by Liz's son Sean.

"Sure. There are bananas in the bowl."

Ewan looked wordlessly at his father.

"There are crisps in the cupboard," Finn said.

"Take a banana too!" Bernie called out, smiling when her son yanked two from the bunch and shoved them into his pocket. Weren't children strange little things? Annoying, yes, and smelly and they covered your house in plastic tat. But then they gave you a look and it was like in the whole world there was nothing more important than this small human being.

"Doesn't it worry you that someone is going around killing our kids' teachers?" Bernie asked Finn, clicking the kettle on for herself.

"One teacher. It's hardly a trend. And I don't know why you're that bothered. He didn't seem like a nice guy."

"You never met him, did you?"

"Yeah, a couple of times. When I was working on the roof."

Bernie spun around to stare at him.

"You never told me that!"

Finn held his hands up to ward her off. "I didn't know you cared."

"Well, I do. Tell me everything."

Her husband shrugged. "I mean, there's not much to tell. He never offered us a cuppa, that's for sure. Not like the other teachers."

Bernie tried not to show her frustration. "Anything else?"

"That woman they arrested. Niamh something. She was always following him around."

"Did you get the feeling she was going to do something?"

"Like she was suddenly going to stab him or bash him over the head with a hockey stick? Nah, she just seemed a bit of a drip. Probably still has her teddy bear. That sort of person."

"That's what I thought," Bernie said. "Anything else?"

"Well, there was one thing. But it's probably nothing."

"Yes?"

Finn shuffled his feet. He was the sort of person who hated gossip. Which Bernie approved of in general, but was not enjoying in this specific case.

"I think he was in trouble with his girlfriend. That Sharon that works in the shoe shop."

Bernie tried not to look too disappointed. "We know about

her. She's got an alibi. Plus, they broke up months ago."

"Really? It was only last week that I saw her up at the school."

"Are you sure?"

"Aye. Some of the young lads thought she was a bit tasty. Not my type of course," Finn said, giving her a grin.

"Better not have been. Go on then, what was she up to?"

"Having a right barny with Jones, by the looks of things. She was waiting for him in her car at the end of school and she sort of pounced on him when he came out. He looked pretty peed off."

"Did you hear what she was saying to him?"

"No. I was on the roof, remember? But she was waving her arms around a lot. Like you do when you are mad at me."

"Huh." Now this was interesting. It proved what Mary had suspected. Sharon had been holding back on them.

"You weren't into that Mr Jones yourself were you? You seem a bit obsessed with the whole thing."

Bernie reached up and kissed Finn on the lips. "Don't be silly. You know I never wanted anyone else."

"Okay then," he said, giving her a lopsided grin. Then he opened the fridge.

Never wanted anyone else, Bernie thought as he took out another beer. And that's the problem.

Chapter 57: Mary

Mary drove towards town with the radio on full blast, playing nineties cheese. She had decided to leave Matt at the house by himself with the kids. Mainly because if she stayed around him any longer she wouldn't be able to resist smacking him across the face.

After she had told him repeatedly that she would not be taking him back, her soon-to-be ex-husband had deposited himself on the sofa and commandeered the remote. It was at that point that Mary suggested he spend some alone time with the kids and handed over a menu for the local pizza delivery place. And forty pounds in cash from her WWC earnings to pay for the food. She had made the mistake of handing her bank card over to Matt before, but it was not one she would repeat.

She had started out with no plan of where she was going. Perhaps she would get a fancy coffee somewhere. Mary didn't actually like coffee very much, but she always felt a bit awkward ordering a tea in the hipster cafes that had sprung up around Invergryff. Maybe some kind of Mocha and then it would taste like dessert.

As she drove past the high street, she had a sudden flash of inspiration. She would go and see Sharon from the shoe shop again. Mary was certain that the woman hadn't told her everything about Sam Jones. Maybe she could find out something important, and then she would have an excuse to call Constable Walker.

Not that she was interested in him, of course. It was just that she wanted to apologise about the whole Matt situation. That was all. Definitely nothing more to it.

She drove past the shoe shop and was irritated to see that it had already shut. After pulling into a parking space she called Bernie.

"Hi, I was thinking I might call in to see Sharon from the shoe shop, but it is shut. I don't suppose you know where she lives."

"No. But I bet you Annie knows. I'll call her. Oh, and you should ask Sharon about her visit to the school last week."

"She was at the school?"

"According to Finn she had a right go at Sam Jones. Hang on a second, I'm going to try and get through to Annie."

Mary sorted through her various social media accounts while she was waiting. Nothing but messages trying to get her to invest in cryptocurrency or encouraging her to lengthen a part of her anatomy that she did not possess. She deleted them all.

"You still there?" Bernie asked a couple of minutes later.

"Yes."

"I couldn't get hold of Annie, but then I remembered that one of my sisters, Cathy, used to work with Maggie Pearson in the knicker department of M&S before she went to manage the shoe shop. Cathy had a number for Maggie so I called her just there. She gave me the address."

Mary keyed it into her satnav as Bernie read it out. "Thanks. So Maggie just gave you the address?"

"Course she did, once I told her that I'd heard she was using her staff discount to buy shoes for someone who was not her husband. Purple loafers, so Cathy said, absolutely outrageous."

"Thanks, Bernie," Mary said and she hung up before Bernie could go down that particular rabbit hole.

After a brief pit stop at a local bakery, Mary turned up Right Said Fred and drove towards the address on the satnav.

Sharon stayed in a flat in a building that had seen better days. It was probably once the poster child for modern living, around about the sixties, but a total lack of upkeep since then had left it with an air of damp and neglect.

Mary made her way past a dozen wheelie bins in a rainbow of colours, all piled high with additional black bin bags, before she got to the door.

When she looked at the entry system for number thirty-seven, she was momentarily stuck. There was no listing for Macdonald. Instead, there were four names. Mr and Mrs Choudhry were flat one, M Macintosh in flat two, S Smelter and finally someone curiously listed as P Grant/Nails by Priya.

Mary rang Bernie again. "I thought Sharon's last name was Macdonald?"

"It is," Bernie replied.

"There's no Macdonald listed. There is an S Smelter though."

"Is that flat three?"

"Yes."

"Then it must be her."

"Maybe she changed her name or something? Was she married before?"

"Why don't you ask her?" Bernie snapped. "Didn't you go round to her house to interview her in the first place?"

"Good point," Mary said and hung up. She wondered for a brief moment what it would be like to be as on-the-ball as Bernie. Life would probably run more smoothly, but would it be a little less fun? Mary decided to tell herself that was true.

"Hello?"

It was definitely Sharon's voice that answered the buzzer.

"It's Mary Plunkett. I bought you an éclair. Can I come up?"

There was a pause, then Sharon said: "I'm kind of busy."

Ahah! Mary thought. The woman was certainly hiding something. "I'll only be a minute. Oh, and it's pistachio and rose water."

"All right then."

Glad that she thought to splash out a staggering three quid on one éclair, Mary climbed the stairs to the third floor.

Even though she knew it was coming, Mary had to stifle a cough as the wave of smoke hit her on entering Sharon's flat.

266

Apart from a couple of cigarettes bummed off friends when she was a teenager, Mary had never smoked and her lungs were telling her to get the hell out of the flat.

Sharon was wearing one of those giant sweatshirts that came down to her knees. "Heating's not working," she said as she showed Mary into the living room.

It was Baltic in there, but at least the open window gave a little respite from the smoke. Mary positioned herself in a chair right below it and wrapped her coat firmly around her body.

"I just wanted to ask you a couple more questions, if that's okay?"

"I guess," Sharon said. "I don't see what else I can tell you."

"Well, I heard that you went up to the school last week."

Sharon glanced down at the floor. "Must have been someone else."

"Not according to my sources," Mary replied, feeling very much like Columbo. "You were seen having a row with Mr Jones."

"I did go and have a word with him. He still had some of my things and I wanted to get them back."

"What things?"

"Oh, some clothes. Nothing important, but I hated the idea of them still being at his place."

Liar, Mary thought. Sharon was not the sort of woman that would wait for months before getting her clothes back from an ex-boyfriend. But was she the sort of person to murder him?

"That explains it then," Mary said, not wanting to put the woman on her guard. She glanced around the room. It had an air of neglect, with no pictures on the wall and only a few photos in glittery frames, mainly of Sharon when she was around ten years younger.

And there it was, right on the mantelpiece. The picture wasn't even in a nice frame, only a cheap cardboard thing that said 'Memories of Blackpool'.

It wouldn't stand up in court, but Mary was prepared to swear that the woman in the picture with her arm around Sharon was the same one from the grainy CCTV at the pub the night Jones was killed.

"That's a lovely picture," Mary said. "I've always fancied going to Blackpool."

Sharon glanced up at the photograph, and Mary could have sworn that she flinched.

"Yeah, it's a good laugh. Listen, I've got to get going." She stood up and practically strong-armed Mary to the door.

"I'll be in touch," Mary said as the door shut behind her.

It was quiet in the close, but Mary could feel that Sharon was standing just on the other side of the door. It was an unsettling feeling. She wasn't sure what to do. Obviously, she wanted to go see Sharon's sister immediately, but she didn't even know where she lived. For some reason, she found herself dialling Constable Walker's number.

Chapter 58: Walker

Back at the police station, Walker was staring at his computer screen when his phone rang. It was Mary Plunkett. Walker stared at it for a moment. Should he answer it? Probably not.

"Hello?"

"Hi, it's Mary. Plunkett. Um, from the Wronged Women's Co-operative."

Walker could feel his eyebrows settle into the usual lowered position they went to whenever he tried to have a conversation with the woman. "From the what?"

"Oh, I hadn't told you what we're called, had I? It's the name of our investigation agency."

Walker pinched the bridge of his nose. He should have followed his instincts not to answer.

"Right. Of course it is. Sorry, did you want something?"

"It's just… I wanted to tell you about Matt."

"This would be the ex-husband that I assaulted in your back garden," Walker said, cringing at the memory.

"He's not going to do anything about that, don't worry. I just wanted to let you know that he's not staying. I mean, in my house. He's actually booked a Travelodge with the kids for a couple of days. You should have heard them on the phone earlier, they think it's the Ritz or something. They were jumping on the beds and everything."

"I don't think they allow that at the Ritz," Walker replied. He checked his watch. "Was there anything else you wanted?"

"Oh, yes, that was why I was calling. I think I've cracked the case."

"What?"

"Sharon has a sister. The one with the chippie."

"That would be Sharon from the shoe shop. The one that went out with Sam Jones."

"Correct. Thing is, I was just at Sharon's flat and her sister looks exactly like your woman from the pub. The picture in the *Gazette*."

"It wasn't the clearest picture."

"Right. But the thing is, in the picture she was wearing the same coat."

Walker leaned forward. "Are you sure?"

"Well, it's a beige raincoat, so I guess there's a few about, but it's a hell of a coincidence, isn't it?"

It was too early to get excited, but Walker could feel his interest building. It was a long shot, but maybe it was worth investigating.

"Listen, I want you to make sure you stay out of this. In fact, I want you to stay in your house. Don't leave until I tell you to, all right?"

"I don't think you can tell me to do that, can you?"

"No," Walker said, reaching for his keys. "But I can ask. Seriously, Mary, let me do my job."

"Fine. As long as you admit that I cracked the case."

"If everything you told me just now is true, then maybe you did. I don't suppose you know the reason why Sharon's sister might have wanted to kill Sam Jones?"

"Not yet, but I'm working on it."

Walker pressed his phone to his ear while he made his way out of the police station.

"Working on it from home, I hope."

"Sure. Look, you don't have to worry about me. I mean, I've got the kids to sort out so I'm hardly going to have time to interfere, am I?"

"Hmmn."

"I'll just do a little internet research. At least I've already done the washing, Thank Gonzo."

It was so weird that Walker missed a step on the stairs and nearly clattered all the way to the bottom. "Why did you say that?"

"Say what?"

"Thank Gonzo. Wasn't he in the Muppets?"

"I didn't say that, did I?"

"You definitely did."

"Oh." The voice on the phone paused. "It's a weird habit I've got into. I don't even realise I'm doing it anymore. The old school the kids were at had a teacher that was quite, you know, god-fearing. She used to think anytime the kids said something like 'oh god' it was swearing. So I tried to get into the habit of using other things. Like old movies and TV shows I like. Hence, thank God became thank Gonzo."

"You are kind of a strange adult, aren't you?" Walker said, but he softened it with a grin that she couldn't see.

"I guess so."

Walker hung up the call. He turned to Neil who was typing something into his laptop.

"Fancy some chips?"

Chapter 59: Liz

"I wonder if we could have a five minute break?" Liz said, using the most reasonable tone she could muster. "I would like the chance to go over the data myself."

"I don't see how that is going to help us," Phil said, looking a little nervous for the first time.

"But surely I have as much of a right as anyone to speak in this meeting? And I cannot do so without all the facts."

Forbes cleared his throat. "I do think it would be quicker to let Mr Hornby finish."

Liz had never realised that being so angry could actually make you feel dizzy. She slammed a hand down on the table.

"I think that five minutes is hardly a lot to ask. Or is there a particular reason that you won't let the only senior female, not to mention person of colour in the room have a chance to establish the facts."

There was a moment of shocked silence.

"Well, perhaps we could allow you five minutes," Joan from HR said with a warning glance at her colleagues.

"I never thought you would be the sort of person to play the race card," Phil said, in the sort of whisper that everyone could hear.

Liz should have felt annoyed, but she was soaring too high for the little man to bother her. "Well, Phil, I felt that I didn't have much of a choice. Seeing as you had already played the dick card."

"Please!" Mr Oliver threw up his hands. "Let's not let this get unpleasant."

Liz was already on her feet, her bag with the folder Amy had prepared for her in her hand. "Five minutes," she said as the door slammed shut behind her.

It was both the longest and the shortest five minutes of her life. Sat on a toilet seat in the ladies loo – it was closer to the meeting room than her office – Liz scanned through the documents as fast as she could. She was terrified of going so fast she might miss something important, but she needed to be sure of herself. Phil had been so convinced he was going to succeed, it would be her word against his. She couldn't afford a single mistake. She phoned Bernie.

"Need help quick," Liz said. "Do you still know someone in Tavistock Estate Agents?" She was pleased she had been able to remember the name of the website she had seen Phil looking at the other day. Hopefully he wasn't just browsing.

Bernie thank goodness didn't bother with small talk. "Yes."

"I need to know about Phil Hornby. Has he bought or sold anything through them recently?"

"On it."

Bernie clicked off the call. Two minutes left. Liz flicked through the sheets, taking a couple of notes, trying to see if the dates meant that...

Her phone buzzed with a message from Bernie. It was a web link to the estate agents' listings and a couple of lines of text.

"Yes!" Liz shouted in relief. She went to type something in reply, then noticed the time. Her five minutes were up.

"Thanks for waiting," Liz said as she slipped back into the room. "I just had to double-check a couple of things."

"I really do have to be back in Glasgow in an hour," Mr Forbes said, straightening his collar. "I'm meeting with three city councillors."

"That's nice," Liz said, aware that that was probably not the correct response, but not caring anyway. "Would you like to hear what I found out?"

Forbes sighed. "Just make it quick."

"I went over the data that Phil sent me, and I have to say he did a thorough job."

"Thanks."

"He was right about the problems between the open documents and the master files. I started with the Bloom case, but the thing is, it wasn't just the one file that was corrupted. Once I started looking there were irregularities in a number of files. I went back over the last two years, and it kept happening again and again. Luckily for us, Phil had already identified all these occasions. I only had to find the pattern."

"You see," Liz said, pointing at the laptop. "Each access point is timestamped. With the date, time and the user name of the person that accessed the spreadsheet. It wasn't difficult to find out who AW was."

Amy's mouth turned into a perfect 'o' shape. "It wasn't me!"

"Amy White. I'm sorry, but those are the initials on the system."

Mr Oliver cleared his throat. "We suspected as much. Phil had pointed out these initials, but I had rather hoped you might come up with a different theory. What do you have to say for yourself, Amy?"

"I didn't do it!" The young woman balled up a tissue and pressed it against her eyes.

"If I might be allowed to add a few more points," Liz said.

"Sure."

"Once I had found the initials, I kept thinking about the logins. Each one with time accessed and a unique set of initials. Each one at the same time. The thing about Amy is that she goes out every day at three fifteen to get a coffee from the cart downstairs. And look at the access times. They are all just after quarter past three but before half past. Someone used Amy's login, knowing that she would be out at those times."

"Wait…" Phil said, half-getting up from his chair.

"Amy was just an easy person to pin this on. What you should be looking for, Mr Forbes, is someone who knew how to mess with the user access names."

"Wouldn't that be your department," Phil said, his tone icy.

"Yes, it is. Only I didn't do it. But I knew that Phil was more than capable of doing it."

"That's a wild accusation," Phil said, looking pointedly at Joan.

"Nobody is accusing anyone of anything today –" Joan began before Liz cut her off.

"Sorry, but the thing is, I knew that Phil could change the user access names. And the reason that I knew is that last Christmas he showed me how to do it."

"Come again?" Forbes asked.

"The first instance you found of files being tampered. I had been working sixteen hour days, trying to get enough time off so that I could have Christmas with my kid. I was tired and stupid and I messed up. You can see on the document that there's an error at the bottom of the page. The bank loan. I miscalculated the interest on the loan and I had told the client the wrong figure. I cost them probably a six figure sum before I realised. I knew that it would look terrible when someone worked out it was my mistake. So I asked Phil for help and he told me how I could cover it up. And I did. I took money from the following month and under-reported it so that the figures worked out. No one even noticed."

"This is all nonsense," Phil grunted.

"That's bordering on fraud," Ben Forbes said, as if Liz didn't already know.

"And a sackable offence," Joan added.

"I know. You can sack me soon enough. But it shows that the files can be manipulated. And if we look at the data again we can see a seven figure sum that has been carefully moved around different accounts. So carefully that it all appears to have been put back. Apart from about half a million pounds that doesn't seem to be accounted for. Unless you look at the person doctoring the files. The person who has just put down a large deposit on a house in Edinburgh."

"What? How can you know that?"

Liz just smiled.

"Well, this puts rather a different spin on things. I think Philip, you and I should have a little chat next door."

"You bastard!"

Before Liz or anyone else could move, Amy lunged across the table and – with an uppercut that Tyson Fury would have been proud of – thumped him one right on the bridge of the nose. Blood sprayed everywhere and Liz heard bone crack.

"Aah!" Phil cried, cradling his battered face.

Amy gave Liz a thumbs up, and she couldn't help but return it. Then she picked up her laptop and left the room.

Chapter 60: Bernie

Annie wasn't answering the phone. She was probably just out at bingo, or getting her nails done. Even so, Bernie had decided to visit her. Just in case. It only took five minutes to get to the care home, if you ignored the least important of the road signs.

Soon enough, Bernie was outside Annie's room. She knocked on the door, and was instantly cheered when she heard a voice say come in.

But once inside Bernie saw that there was no one in Annie's chair. Instead, there was a young girl making her bed with neat hospital corners.

"Hi, I'm Kayleigh. I don't think we've met."

"Where's Annie?"

Bernie knew the answer before the woman opened her mouth.

"She died just a couple of hours ago."

"Why didn't anyone tell me?"

The girl shuffled her feet. "I'm sorry, I don't know your name."

"It's Bernie Paterson."

"Ah right, the nurse. I didn't think you were on duty today."

"I'm not. I was just popping in to see... Never mind. Where's

Lucy?"

"She's off sick, her son's got the flu."

"You should have called her. After you called me."

The girl's mouth turned downwards. "Sorry, I didn't know. I thought the procedure was to let the management know, then the next of kin."

"Well, yes, that's the procedure," Bernie said, but didn't add, *but not for Annie, you little fool.*

"Sorry again," she sniffed. "It's the first one I've seen. A dead body, I mean."

"Won't be the last," Bernie replied, but she put her hand on the young woman's shoulder. It wasn't her fault, after all, that Annie McGillivray was dead, even if Bernie felt like it was. It wasn't anyone's fault. That was always the tragedy of it all.

"Why don't you go and get a cup of tea," Bernie added. "I'll finish tidying up here."

"All right. I better give you this though, before I forget."

Kayleigh held out a letter.

"What's that?"

"Annie left it for you."

"Of course she did. Thanks."

Bernie took the letter in her hand and turned it over. It was written in slightly shaky handwriting, but still perfectly neat. A teacher to the end, weren't you Mrs McGillivray, she thought.

To Bernie Paterson

I'm afraid when you get this, I'll be gone. I've taken a couple extra of those lovely pills that the doctor sorted out for me the other day. I'd much rather that than spend the next week falling away like so many here do. We've seen enough of it, haven't we pet?

Now, I want you to take that Boston fern I've been growing, and put it in the staff room. I know that Lucy likes it and she'll be made up. I've also left my wool jacket to Mrs Wright because she always admired it. All the real valuables are in the will, so I'll let the lawyers sort that out. They ought to do, the amount I've paid them.

Now Bernie, I will only say this once, and you've got to listen to me because I'm dead. You're the most capable, cleverest, brilliant woman I have ever met. And that is the problem. You have never learned how to rely on other people. You think this is a weakness, right?

I know you do. We're very alike, you and I. Why do you think I never married? Anyway, it took me until my nineties to realise that I'd got it all wrong. Yes, I might know how to use an oxford comma, but, I never learned to share. I never learned that when you let people into your life, it doesn't make you weaker, it makes you stronger.

This is an old woman's rambling way of saying, keep hold of your friends. Don't shut them out because they don't live up to your expectations: they never will.

I have left my house and what little money the care home hasn't swallowed to the WWC. I put it in my will last month, and I even sent a letter to those management know-it-alls at the home to say that I was doing so of my own free will. Just in case they come knocking on your door all suspicious. So you and the other woman will have a place to meet for as long as you need it. And I hope you need it a damned long time. I'm proud of you, Bernie. That's a fact.

And I know you won't let me down. That's because if you do you know that I'll be winging my way down from heaven to kick your bony behind.

Annie

Well, that was that, Bernie thought. So long, Annie McGillivray. She should be happy really. Annie giving them the house meant that the WWC could keep going, become a career rather than a hobby. But all she could feel was the loss.

Pull yourself together, Bernadette, she told herself. If Annie was to have a legacy then maybe it would be that Bernie did what she was told, for once. Perhaps it was time to reach out, let other people help her for once.

Or maybe she should solve Sam Jones's murder all on her own and rub it in that cocky young police officer's face. That would feel pretty damn good too.

Chapter 61: Mary

Now that Mary had decided to do a little breaking and entering, she was lacking her partner in crime. For once, Bernie wasn't answering her phone. Mary tapped her thumb against her front teeth. What should she do?

Of course, she should be at home. Constable Walker had explicitly told her not to get involved. But he didn't actually have any legal powers to stop from her leaving the house. Mary had done an internet search, just to make sure.

Obviously, what she wanted to do was to catch the murderer, get them to confess and present them to Constable Walker who would be ever so grateful. But Mary had the feeling that maybe that wouldn't be quite as easy as Jessica Fletcher made it look.

If only Bernie was here with the key. Mary took a peek at the house. She had parked the car two streets away but in a position where she could still see Jones's front door. There didn't seem to be anyone around. No police cars in front, in any case. Well, at least she knew the way to get around the back.

She waited another five minutes but finally, she couldn't resist. In a matter of moments she had climbed out of the car and let herself into Sam Jones's back garden before she'd had time to think too hard about it.

The garden looked the same as last time, just as neglected. Mary glanced up at next door's windows, but she couldn't see any sign of Geoff Bilsland. She gave him a jaunty wave anyway, just in case he was thinking she shouldn't be there. Which of course she shouldn't.

Where the hell was Bernie? Mary had sent her three text messages and two emails just in case she didn't have reception. Honestly, the way the woman talked about the WWC like it was her life's vocation, but then when she was needed she was off having her nails done or something.

She peeked into the garden shed again, but it didn't look like anyone had touched it since the last time. Maybe she should just check the back door? And the windows? If any were open, it was hardly breaking and entering, was it?

Mary stood outside, shuffling from one foot to the other. She should wait for the others. Of course she should. But then, wouldn't it be nice to prove to them that silly little Mary Plunkett was just as capable of taking the initiative as they were?

She imagined Matt's face when she called him to tell him that they had solved a murder. Constable Walker's lips curling into a small smile when she presented him with the case all wrapped up in a bow. Perhaps they could celebrate with a drink somewhere. Maybe a cup of tea and a slice of Victoria sponge.

Anyway. Time to do something. Her hand was on the doorknob of the back door before she realised it. She said a silent prayer to any gods that might be listening and turned the handle.

It opened.

She was so shocked she just looked at the open door for several seconds. Apart from anything else, she thought, Mary might have to rethink her atheism. Before she could chicken out, she slipped into the kitchen and pulled the door shut behind her.

Had the police left the door unlocked? It seemed unlikely, but maybe they had. She started to look around the kitchen which was white, shiny and empty. Sam Jones hadn't been much of a cook, by the looks of things. She opened the fridge. Some seriously questionable milk and some tins of pickles and hot sauce. Nothing else.

Mary went to open some of the covers but then she stopped. Had she heard something? No, it was just her imagination. Then she heard a crash from the front room.

Mary held her breath. Of course that was why the back door was open, someone was already in the house! She was torn between frustration that something so simple hadn't occurred to her and a pure animal fear of being discovered somewhere she wasn't allowed to be.

The layout of the house meant that there was barely anywhere to hide. From the kitchen she could go up the stairs, but if anyone came out of the living room she would walk right into them. Mary turned to the back door. Her best chance of getting away was to simply go back the way she came.

But what would she learn then? Because now she really, really wanted to know who it was that was in Sam Jones's house. And whether they had any more right to be there than she did.

Moving as quickly as she could while trying not to make a

sound, Mary crept out of the kitchen and moved towards the stairs. There was a woman's handbag just inside the front door and a coat hanging up on the pegs. Mary half-crouched as she moved past the doorway to the living room, but thankfully the door was hung so that the person on the other side couldn't see her at this angle. She moved towards the stairs, then pressed herself against the wall and went up them as quickly as she dared.

Unlike her own house, the stairs didn't creak and she somehow made it into the bedroom without any noise from down below. She had done it! Although now she was trapped upstairs, Mary realised, unless she wanted to chance moving past the living room once more. The bedroom was small with nowhere to hide apart from the fitted wardrobes.

So she climbed in. She squatted down underneath Sam Jones's shirts and wondered what the hell she should do next.

Her phone buzzed. Crap! She just had to hope the sound hadn't been audible to the person downstairs.

Mary squished herself further into the cupboard. She pulled her phone out of her pocket and saw that it was from Walker.

Where are you?

Now was probably not the time to tell him. Mary thought that Walker might be kind of annoyed if she let on that she was hiding in the victim's wardrobe.

Chapter 62: Liz

Liz cleared her desk in less time than it had taken the HR woman to plug up Phil's broken nose. There was still some shouting going on in the meeting room, but Amy had already agreed to a twenty per cent pay rise and Phil had agreed not to prosecute her for assault. Liz had no doubt that the business would find some way of avoiding reporting Phil to the authorities. He would probably just be quietly retired. All's well that ends well, right? But at least she would be able to take the image of Amy's fist connecting with his clammy face with her to the grave.

"Can I have a word, Liz?" It was Mr Oliver, standing awkwardly in the doorway.

"I was just leaving. I'll hand in my laptop and things tomorrow."

"I was wondering if you might reconsider. Perhaps you might like to stay on with the company."

Liz blinked. "What?"

"You can have Phil's job. I never really liked the little squirt anyway. He always cheated when he landed in the rough."

And he stole hundreds of thousands of pounds, Liz added silently.

"Look, you made a mistake," Mr Oliver continued. "But you owned up to it in the end. And, frankly, we need someone in this office who actually knows what the hell they are doing. We'd love you to step up to the plate."

"Right. I guess that would be the sensible option," Liz said. She looked down at her uncomfortable shoes.

"So we're agreed?"

"I'm afraid not."

Mr Oliver's smile faltered. "I don't understand…"

"It's about time I did something for myself. I'm not too sure what that is yet, but I know that it isn't here. Consider this my notice."

There should have been some sort of Aretha Franklin song playing as she walked out of the building. Or at least a Dolly Parton. But the moment was sweet enough as it was. It was only slightly ruined by her slipping on her steps in her high boots and twisting her ankle.

Liz hobbled back to her car and sat in the driver's seat with her eyes closed, head leaning back against the headrest. She should be feeling panicked, wondering about how to explain everything to Dave, but although he would be shocked, she knew he would support her decision.

As she tried to savour the moment, Liz became aware that something was digging into her back. She reached into her jeans pocket and pulled out a plastic object. Crap, the memory stick that she'd brought to the school. The one that she had used to save Niamh Devon and Sam Jones's files. With all the work drama she hadn't even had the chance to look at it.

Liz pulled out her laptop and plugged the drive in. Maybe there would be something that could clear Niamh Devon on there. Plus, the longer she spent scrolling through files the more time she could spend avoiding her work situation.

First, she brought up Niamh Devon's documents. There weren't actually that many. As a teaching assistant, she didn't have to do the same prep work as the teachers did. There was a folder of payslips that Liz clicked through, but apart from seeing how woeful her wage was, it didn't tell her anything new about Niamh.

Next, she clicked on Sam Jones's documents. Unlike Niamh's, the teacher's folders were full of files, mainly images and word documents for use in the classroom. She clicked quickly through these, but there was nothing that caught her eye. Then she spotted a folder of internet downloads.

Again, it was mostly information for lessons, maths challenges, that sort of thing. But one file caught her eye. It was a series of emails that he had backed up on the computer, presumably because he thought they were important.

Liz opened the emails and scanned them as fast as she could. They were a conversation between Jones and a solicitor, and they seemed to concern the details of a house sale. According to the emails, Jones had bought his house from a Mr Smelter, and got it at a decent price, by the looks of it.

Hang on, Liz thought, opening a web browser on the laptop. The emails said that he paid only a hundred grand. That seemed like a very good price. Maybe too good to be true?

Five minutes searching on house selling websites later, Liz was certain of it. Three other houses on the same estate had sold for almost double that price. So why had Jones paid so little?

She pulled out her phone and dialled her friend's number. The first time there was no answer, then she finally picked up.

"Bernie! Where are you, I've been trying to get in touch."

"Can't talk right now." Bernie's voice was little more than a whisper.

"Why? What's going on?"

"I'm at Sam Jones's house. And I'm pretty sure your timid little friend Mary Plunkett has just let herself in the back door."

"What?"

"Yep. She phoned me but I couldn't answer. I was on the phone myself to Annie's next of kin."

Liz closed her eyes for a second. "Do you mean that…"

"Yes. Passed away today. And I'm going to be bloody upset about that when I get the chance. Right now I think we need to focus on Mary. Because the thing is, she's not the only one in the house."

Liz was already turning the key in the ignition. "I'll be over right away."

Chapter 63: Bernie

Bernie had spotted Mary's car as soon as she'd driven to Sam Jones's place. It wasn't hard, it was a good ten years older than every other car on the street and was full of car seats and biscuit crumbs. It also had a sticker on the back window that said 'My other car's the Enterprise NCC-1701' for some reason that Bernie couldn't fathom.

However, there was a car parked right outside Sam Jones's house that Bernie didn't recognise. It wasn't Geoff Bilsland's, because she knew that he'd had to give up driving while he was waiting to get his cataracts done. And it didn't seem like it would be one of the neighbours, as they all had driveways. It was one of those funny modern minis that looked like someone had blown it up in a photo editing program. All bulges in the wrong places.

Bernie had left her own car around the corner, not worrying too much if she was spotted. After all, it was looking more and more likely that Mary might need her help, and if she was going to go storming into Sam Jones's house there wasn't much point in hiding the fact that she was there.

Of course, if she'd arrived five minutes earlier she would have been able to stop Mary going in. As it was she had been just in time to see through the fence the curious image of Mary slipping in through the back door.

Now Bernie was looking at the front of the house and trying to work out what to do. The curtains were closed in the front room. Had they been before? Bernie couldn't swear to it, but she thought they might have been open. She leaned against a lamppost on the other side of the street and pretended to check something on her phone.

She could knock on the door. That would be the obvious thing to do. But what if Mary was in trouble? Bernie wasn't often troubled by introspection, but she did wonder if maybe she hadn't made the whole private investigation business sound a little less dangerous than it actually was. If Mary Plunkett was about to get her brains bashed in, leaving her four children practically orphans (Bernie obviously wasn't counting the clearly feckless ex-husband as a parent) then maybe she would feel a little guilty about that. So she needed a more subtle approach, a way to get into the house without alerting anyone inside.

But that wasn't a problem. Because Bernie had a key. She felt in her coat pocket and sure enough, the key that she had 'borrowed' from under the plant pot was still there. The only issue would be finding a way to get in that wouldn't alert everyone inside.

"Psst!" Bernie turned around to see Liz standing behind a large oak tree that stood a few houses away from Sam Jones's house. She hurried over to her, noting that every person on the street must have noticed them by now.

"What are you doing?" Bernie said, unable to stop herself from whispering.

"Hiding," Liz said, her eyes flicking to Sam Jones's house. "I didn't want to park outside so I'm over on the main road."

"One better than Mary, then," Bernie said, pointing out the other woman's car. "But I don't think standing behind this tree is going to make us look anything other than bloody suspicious."

"I thought I was doing okay," Liz said with a pout.

"You're about as inconspicuous as any other black woman dressed in a suit in a small town in Scotland," Bernie said, her attention back on the house with its closed curtains.

"I take your point," Liz said. "So what's going on over there?"

"Not sure. Do you know whose car that is in front of Sam Jones's place?"

Liz shook her head. "No."

"It's not Sharon's," Bernie said. "I'm pretty sure she doesn't have a car. That flat she stays in doesn't have any parking. Oh, and Mary was telling me something earlier which didn't make any sense. She said that Sharon's last name used to be Smelter."

"Smelter?" Liz reached out and gripped Bernie's elbow. "Are you sure?"

"Ow. Yes. What's the problem?"

"I think I know what's going on. Or, at least, part of it. The person who used to live in Sam Jones's house was a Mr Smelter."

"Sharon's father?"

"Yes. And that's not the most interesting part. It turns out that —"

"Hang on, there's someone in the bedroom."

A face appeared at the window, and it wasn't Mary's.

"Who is that?"

"I thought it might be Sharon, but the hair is different."

"Did you notice something?" Liz asked.

"What?"

"She looked kind of like the woman in the CCTV photos."

"Really?"

Liz grabbed her arm. "You don't think Mary is still in there, do you? That woman could be Jones's murderer!"

Bernie sighed. "Then that's probably exactly where Mary is. Let's go."

Chapter 64: Walker

Constable Walker had turned on the police car's siren, but for once he wasn't particularly enjoying the experience of racing through traffic with his flashing lights on. Normally, like most police officers, he found a tiny thrill in being allowed to drive faster than everyone else. It was his inner child, he supposed, or maybe it was just something that no one ever grew out of. But today, when someone he cared about might be in danger, he felt no thrill. Only a knot of stress in his stomach that wouldn't go away.

Neil had been looking bored in the office, so Walker had offered him a trip to the local chippy. It had only taken the offer of a fish special to tempt him along. The Sergeant had been more than happy to go to the chippy with him for a bit of reconnaissance work.

"The Fish Plaice?" Neil had said when Walker told them where he wanted to go. "That's my local. Best batter in Invergryff."

"Do you know the woman that owns it?"

"Kitty something. Not really, I don't exactly stay for the small talk."

"Her sister is Sharon Macdonald."

"Sharon from the shoe shop?" Neil asked. "The one that went out with Sam Jones?"

"Bingo. Now, Kitty gave Sharon an alibi for the night that

Jones was killed. But my source seems to think that Kitty herself is a pretty good match for Sam Jones's friend in the pub."

Neil chewed this over for a few minutes. "All right, but why would you kill your sister's ex-boyfriend?"

"I have no idea. But it's got to be worth checking out. Even if it's nothing, we'll get a fish supper out of it."

"Then count me in."

It was only a fifteen minute ride from the station and they turned up at the chippy just as it was opening up for evening service.

The tang of vinegar hit their noses as soon as they walked in the door and Walker heard his stomach rumble. There was nothing better than the smell of real chippy chips.

"Is Kitty in?" Walker asked when they walked up to the counter. There was a man serving, a skinny guy with a thin beard.

"Nah, she's not in yet. Normally starts at eight and then does the close."

"Did you work last Thursday night?"

"Yes, and the other policeman already asked me if Sharon was here. She worked the whole night, six until cashing up at near enough half past twelve."

"We know," Neil said, leaning over the counter. "But did anyone ask you about Kitty?"

"Kitty?" The guy should never play poker, Walker thought, as the man's eyes flickered to the floor.

"Yeah, was your boss here on Thursday?"

"Sure she was, same as usual."

"The whole night?"

The man bit his lip. "Look, don't tell her I told you, okay? I need this job."

"Go on," Neil said.

"She opened up at four, but then around seven she said she had to do something. Kitty said that it would be okay as Sharon could cover for her."

"Did she come back?"

"Not until nearly midnight."

Walker wanted to punch the air, but he kept his expression blank. "Why didn't you tell us this earlier?"

"You only asked about Sharon. It wasn't like I was lying."

Walker tapped Neil on the shoulder and they walked out. It might be that the man was covering for his boss, but they didn't have time to worry about that now. Their priority was the murder case and they had just found a gold-plated suspect.

"We should call this into the office," Neil said, already getting his phone out.

"Ask for Macleod. And try and find out Kitty's address."

While Neil was barking into his phone, Walker's personal mobile started to ring. This was unfortunate as he'd forgotten to set it to silent and he had just changed the ringtone to Gangnam Style. Thankfully Neil was too busy updating Macleod to notice.

It was Mary. Walker was relieved when he saw her name pop up. She'd never replied to his message earlier asking where she was, and he'd had a horrible feeling she was meddling in the case.

"Hi," he said.

"Shhh," a whispering voice said on the other end of the line. "Can't talk. I'm at Sam Jones's house."

"What?" Walker couldn't help but raise his voice. Neil looked around in confusion.

"Shhh! Look, Sharon's sister is here."

"What?" Walker said again. He seemed to have lost the ability to form a sentence. "Where are you?"

"In the wardrobe but I think she's coming upstairs. I'm going to leave my phone on in case she confesses."

"Don't you dare move," Walker said, jumping into the front seat of his car. "I'm on my way."

"What's going on?" Neil asked, climbing in next to him.

"It's a long story, but a civilian friend of mine has somehow ended up in Sam Jones's house with our main suspect."

Neil whistled through his teeth. "Christ."

"Yeah. Can you put your phone next to mine and record whatever she says?"

"Sure. I guess we're heading there right now?"

"Yes. We'll call it into HQ on the way, but I'm not sure there will be time for them to send anyone else before all hell breaks loose."

"What exactly is happening here?"

"I'm not a hundred per cent sure, but I think something really, really bad." That was when he turned on the siren.

Chapter 65: Mary

If Mary had been on a certain famous television science fiction show then she would have been firing torpedoes, raising shields and releasing the saucer section. In other words, the moment of catastrophe had arrived.

She knew she was in trouble as soon as the bedroom door opened.

"Who is in here?" A voice asked. It was female, a stranger, and someone who was seriously peed off.

For a few moments, Mary just sat there. At least she had had the foresight to call Walker as soon as the footsteps had started on the stairs. She had slipped her phone into the front pocket of her jeans and wrapped her long cardigan around her so that it didn't leave any obvious outline.

Eventually, unable to bear it any longer, Mary pushed open the wardrobe doors.

"Hello, my name is Mary," she said, considering that it was only polite to introduce yourself to someone when you had just popped out of a wardrobe.

"What the hell were you doing in there?"

"It's sort of a long story. Will we have a cup of tea, Kitty? It is Kitty, isn't it?"

The woman chewed her lip for a moment before nodding. "All right," she said. "I'll make the tea while you explain yourself."

Mary followed Sharon's sister down the stairs. She could see her blond hair was slightly thin on top, and pulled back into a claw clip, but she was more certain than ever that this was the woman from the CCTV images. She was prettier than Sharon, Mary reckoned, and a few years older.

"I'm not sure why I'm making you tea," Kitty said as she clicked on the kettle. "I mean, I don't think you should be here, should you?"

Mary took a deep breath. "I don't mean to be rude, but it sort of feels like you shouldn't be here either," she pointed out, with an apologetic look.

"This was my dad's house," Kitty said, her face pale. "I just wanted to pick up some things that he had left behind, that's all."

"And it's a good opportunity to come back, because the current owner is dead, isn't that right?"

Kitty looked up from the tea things. "Yes, I had heard about that. What a waste."

She passed over a mug of tea. Mary cupped it in her hands, picked it up ready to drink, then paused. Now if this was a vintage crime novel, she thought to herself, the tea would definitely be poisoned. Slowly, she replaced the cup on the table.

"Not thirsty?" Kitty asked.

"Too hot," Mary replied pushing the cup further away. "What exactly was it that you were trying to find of your father's? I imagine that all his things all her long gone."

301

Kitty sniffed. "I don't see that that is any of your business. You're not a copper, that's pretty clear, so why are you here?"

Mary was about to tell her that she was a very brilliant private investigator, when a flash of inspiration struck.

"I was... well, the truth is I was kind of dating Sam."

"You were?"

"Yeah, we met online. We had only had a couple of dates, but I really liked him. Anyway, I was looking for some stuff and I think I might have left it here. Just some clothes, but I would be kind of mortified if anyone found them, so that was why I was in the wardrobe. I had no idea you were in the house too."

Kitty visibly relaxed. "I hate to break it to you, but he kind of dated a lot of people."

"Yeah, I found that out pretty quickly. Turns out he was seeing about three other girls when he was meant to be going out with me. He was a bit of a dick, all things considered."

Kitty smiled agreement.

Mary picked up the cup and pretended to take a sip. "Do you think that's why he was killed?"

"None of my business," Kitty said.

"You know, you kind of look like the woman on the CCTV images," Mary said. It was a risky thing to ask, but she knew that her phone was relaying the whole conversation to Walker, so she wasn't in any danger. Probably. Maybe best not to drink the tea though, just in case.

"Those terrible photos they put in the paper? Jesus, that could be anyone."

"Yeah, I guess so. You never dated him then, Sam Jones I mean?"

"No. My sister went out with him for a while."

"Broke her heart, did he?"

Kitty laughed. "I don't think so. She had more sense than to think the man was going to marry her."

"And you're sure you didn't go out with him that night? It's just... I could have sworn that the pictures on telly looked just like you."

"Sam would know it was me, surely. His girlfriend's sister. Why on earth would he go on a date with me?"

Mary's brows creased. She hadn't thought of that. It would be strange if he didn't recognise his own girlfriend's sister. Unless...

"You recently moved over here from Oban, didn't you? Maybe you had never actually met him. Sam was never that serious about Sharon, at least not as serious as she was about him. Maybe he wasn't that bothered about meeting her family."

Kitty shrugged. "You can believe what you like."

"Of course, he met your dad often enough, didn't he?" Mary said.

The face of the woman changed into something brittle and hard. "Don't talk about my dad."

For the first time, Mary felt like she might have been a bit hasty confronting the woman like this. "Sorry, I didn't mean to upset you."

"Upset me?" Kitty folded her arms. "It seems like you have every intention of upsetting me. I don't think you ever went out with Sam. You seem much too clever to have made that mistake. So I'm going to ask you again, what are you doing here?"

"I… Like I said, I was dating –"

"Liar!"

In one motion, Kitty grabbed the mug and threw it at the window. The window smashed and the mug sailed straight through.

Both women stared at it for a moment, each as shocked as the other.

"Well, that's done it," Kitty said at last. "What the hell am I going to do now?"

Chapter 66: Liz

Bernie had only taken a step towards the house when there was a smash and a sound like a mini explosion from Sam Jones's house. Both women looked up at the sound of breaking glass. Some sort of projectile had flown out of the living room window of the house, landing in pieces on the pavement below.

"Mary!" Bernie shouted, and ran for the door, Liz only a footstep behind her. By the time they got to the house, Bernie was well in front.

"Ten hours a week on the treadmill," Bernie said as she reached the door. "Now where did I put that blooming key?"

Liz bounced from one foot to another while Bernie routed around in her handbag. She tried not to think about what was happening to poor Mary while they were stuck outside. She tried to peer through the window but she didn't want to go too close to the shattered glass.

"Okay, I found it. I don't suppose you've got a weapon on you? A Taser maybe, or one of Annie's bread knives?"

"Jesus, no. I've got a bottle of hand sanitiser. Maybe I could squirt it in her eyes."

"Sounds good. Let's go." Bernie pushed the door open and jumped through. Liz followed so closely behind that she slammed into her back when Bernie ground to a stop. Liz grabbed Bernie's shoulder and peeked around her head to see why she had stopped.

There, sitting on the sofa was Mary and next to her, with her head on their friend's shoulder was Sharon's sister Kitty. She was quietly sobbing while Mary had her arm around her.

"Um, hello?" Bernie, who had for some reason raised her fists like a prize fighter, lowered her hands to her sides.

"Hi," Mary said. "Kitty and I are just having a little chat. Why don't you both sit down?"

Bernie and Liz looked at each other, shrugged, and sat down. Liz wondered if a cup of coffee would be out of the question. Scratch that, a gin would be better. It was turning out to be a very strange day.

"And what were you talking about?" Liz asked, her eyes flicking to the broken window.

"Kitty, do you want to tell them?"

The woman next to Mary shrugged.

"I guess I have to tell people now, don't I? I was just so cross with him," Kitty said, raising her head and showing her red-rimmed eyes to Bernie and Liz. "I wasn't thinking straight. I just wanted him to be sorry for what he did to my sister. That's all. He was such a pig."

"I don't think any of us will argue with that one," Liz said, trying to put the woman at ease.

"Not a good reason to kill him though, was it?" Bernie said and Liz looked at her in horror.

Kitty sat up straight and clenched fists. "How dare you –"

There was the sound of the front door being yanked open. A moment later Constable Walker and a second police officer walked into the room.

"Can we take over from now on please, ladies," he said.

Chapter 67: Bernie

It was getting awfully crowded in the living room of the dead man. Bernie had offered to scoot up for the police officers, but they had chosen to remain standing. Probably an authority thing, although it was true that the leather suite was not particularly comfortable.

"We heard you confess over the phone, Mrs Perrins," Walker said.

"Phone? What phone?"

Mary pulled her mobile out. "Sorry, but I felt I had to record it. Especially if you were going to go crazy and stab me to death. Which you didn't, obviously."

Kitty looked like she wanted to throw something at Mary again, but she contented herself with just giving her a death stare.

"I will be having a word with you later, Mrs Plunkett," the Constable said, and something in his tone told Bernie that it wouldn't be the congratulations that the WWC deserved.

"Let's get her back to the station," the other policeman said. "If you come quietly we won't need any handcuffs, all right, Kitty?"

Kitty, head down, gave a small nod.

"Constable Walker, will you give Ms Perrins the police caution?"

This was the exciting bit, just like on TV when the police would 'read them their rights'. But Bernie found her mind wandering a little while the Sergeant was saying the familiar phrases. There were still too many loose ends, and Bernie hated not knowing things. She was damned if the WWC were going to get this far and the police take away their murderer, only to find out the juicy details afterwards.

"I wonder if you could spare a couple of minutes before you take her to the station," Bernie said, once the little speech was finished. "It's just, there's a couple of things I'd like to ask your prisoner here."

"She is not a prisoner," Walker said. "And I think that…"

"You'd like to talk to us rather than the police officers, wouldn't you, Kitty? I mean, they're men after all. They won't understand why you killed Sam Jones."

"He dumped my sister. I… I got so cross, I wasn't thinking straight, so I killed him."

Bernie gave her the sort of hard smile she reserved for patients who refused to take their medication. "Well, that would be all well and good if you were a deranged baddie on a TV show. I mean, you could even do a maniacal laugh if you like. But the thing is, I don't think you've quite told us the whole story, have you Kitty?"

Kitty folded her arms and said nothing.

"I think Mrs Paterson might have a point," Constable Walker said. "If you had never intended to kill Sam Jones, then why would you have brought a syringe full of morphine with you to the pub?"

Bernie tapped her foot on the floor. "And where would someone that worked in a chippy get hold of morphine? It's a controlled substance."

Kitty kept her head down and said nothing.

"And you said it was administered by syringe?" Bernie asked the Constable.

"Yes."

"Then it must have come from a hospital, otherwise it would be given as tablets. They don't give out intravenous morphine these days." Bernie paused. "Or it was from somewhere like a care home. We have heavy doses of morphine for our clients who are suffering from acute pain. Like your dad would have been, when we treated him. Terminal cancer, wasn't it?"

Liz cleared her throat. "And I've been wondering about this house sale. Your father sold it to Sam Jones while he was ill. Sold it for a very good price, didn't he?"

Kitty sniffed and stood up. "I would like to go now."

"I think maybe you came here looking for Sam Jones's financial records. Something that would give you evidence to show how you might be able to get the money back that your father lost on the sale. I took a look at the financial records for your chippy. You might have the best batter in Invergryff, but you're trading at a loss."

"Best batter in Scotland," Kitty muttered.

"You told me this was all about Sam Jones letting your sister down," Mary added, in a quiet voice. "I don't think it was about women at all, was it, or about Sharon? I think it was all about money and revenge. You took the morphine when your father was dying and saved it, waiting for the moment when you could use it to kill Sam Jones."

There was a moment of silence while each person digested this idea.

"It wasn't just about the money," Kitty said finally. "It was about my dad. He only sold the house to Jones because he said he was going to marry Sharon. That we were all family. Sam Jones conned my dad out of his money when he was dying. Made the end of his life a misery. It was unforgiveable."

"Okay, I think we'll get you down the station now to make your statement," Walker said, gesturing to the door. Kitty followed behind him and the Sergeant came last. Once Kitty was locked in the back of the police car, Constable Walker came back into the house.

"I don't know where to start with you lot," he said, offering them all a particularly stern glare. No wonder Mary fancied him, Bernie thought, he had something of the Mr Darcy about him. The good one done by the BBC, not the rubbish film.

"We only came in because we were concerned about Mary," Liz said.

"And why was Mary in here in the first place?"

Mary herself looked up at the ceiling, as if the chrome light

311

fighting was extraordinarily fascinating. "I suppose I was worried that she might destroy some evidence of something. I wanted to make sure that we caught her in time."

"You should have called me and waited outside! For god's sake, Mary, what would I have done if she'd killed you?"

You could have heard a pin drop, which is a weird expression, and probably not true with modern carpeted floors. Bernie looked from Mary to Walker and back again. Finally Walker found his voice.

"What I mean to say is, if a civilian was killed on my watch, I would have got in a hell of a lot of trouble. I don't know how I'm going to explain all this as it is."

Bernie stepped forward. "I think you should tell them the truth. That the Wronged Women's Co-operative solved the crime and basically saved the day."

Walker stood still, his mouth working as if he was trying to stop the words that wanted to come out. After a few seconds he turned around and marched out of the door, back to the police car. It drove away with no sirens or high-speed cornering. Bernie was disappointed. In that way it was not like the TV at all.

Epilogue

Mary sat on the wall outside the school. It was still ten minutes until the kids came out, but she liked to get there early. Especially when the autumn sun came out like today and made everything seem a little bit cheerier. She had her big coat on and a warm scarf that her mum had knitted so she was cosy and content. What more could anyone want?

It didn't take long for her to recognize the tall figure walking towards her. The uniform kind of made him easy to spot.

"Nice day," Walker said, taking a seat beside her.

"Yes," Mary said. She wasn't sure if he was angry with her or not. She had been brought into the police station to make a statement about the whole revealing-a-murderer-and-getting-them-to-confess thing. She had been left not with the hearty congratulations she had been expecting, but instead with a warning on breaking and entering and interfering with police business. She hadn't even seen Walker there. Instead, she had been interviewed by other police officers who were much less fun.

"We picked up Sharon last night," Walker said. "She'll probably end up with some sort of accessory charge. We think she knew about the morphine at least, although it will be hard to show that she knew Kitty was planning the murder."

"She was though, wasn't she?"

"Oh yes. We have plenty of evidence of premeditation. The

procurator fiscal makes the final decision, of course, but we think we've done a good job of presenting our case."

Mary kicked her legs against the wall.

"You're not saying much," Walker said.

"Well, to be honest, I was kind of waiting for you to say thank you. To the WWC. For solving the case for you."

"Wow. Is that what you think happened?"

"Clearly."

Walker's cheeks turned pink. "The way I see it, you put yourself in danger and I had to come and rescue you."

Mary was so annoyed she had to stand up and face him. "You truly think that's what happened? This isn't a movie and I'm not a damsel in distress. I mean, if anything you're the Princess!"

"What?"

"Yeah, without me to rescue you from your own ignorance, you would never have solved the case."

For a moment, Mary thought that Walker looked mad enough to just turn on his heels and walk away. Then his face softened and he started to laugh.

"You are a completely impossible person, do you know that?"

"It's been said." Mary paused for a second. "Do you know, it's kind of unsatisfying. I mean, I know that Kitty killed Jones and she deserves to go to prison for it, but I feel a bit sorry for her. Jones was a real arse to that family."

"I'm afraid that real police work isn't always as easy as it is on the telly. In real life nothing gets tied up in a bow all neat at the end. There's always another case waiting, another episode spent travelling into the unknown, to boldly go where no one has been before."

Mary looked up in surprise. "You're a Trek fan?"

"Well, I don't know if I'd call myself a fan…" Walker said, a smile curling the corner of his mouth.

Mary took a step towards him, then realised there was a small woman heading towards her.

"Thank you!"

Mary was enveloped in a hug. It took her a few moments to work out who this person was.

"Niamh! It's good to see you. I guess you've been released?"

"Cleared of all charges," the young woman said, bouncing on her toes in excitement. "I got out as soon as they charged that other woman. Back home to the cat. Anyway, I was speaking to Bernie Paterson a minute ago and she said it was all thanks to you. That you found out the real murderer. And I just wanted to say the biggest thank you."

Mary turned a little pink. "Well, you are very welcome."

"Yes. I'm glad you showed those idiots at the police station who the real killer was." At this, she gave Walker a first degree glare, hugged Mary again, then hurried off towards the school.

"Well, that was pretty awesome," Mary said. She turned back to face Walker, who was looking at her with a nervous expression.

He shuffled from one foot to the other. "I want to ask you something. Um. Look, I know your situation is… complicated."

Four kids, an ex-husband that wasn't entirely ex and a job where she pretended she was Nancy Drew? Yep, definitely complicated. Mary just nodded.

"But maybe you would like to grab a cup of tea with me sometime. In a café. Not one that has been made with milk from your fridge."

Mary smiled. She opened her mouth to answer him but then the school bell rang.

"I'd love to," Mary said, "Maybe not this week, or next. Maybe not for a while yet. But once I get my life sorted out, can I give you a call?"

He started to reply, but she was already walking towards the school, where a group of red-headed children were running her way. Life would never be simple, she thought as she drew the kids into her arms for a cuddle. But it was certainly more interesting than it used to be.

Afterword

I hope you enjoyed the first book from the Wronged Women's Co-operative. This book has been floating around in my head for a little while. I wanted to write something where mums get to take centre stage, rather than fading into the background like we so often tend to do. I have fallen in love with Bernie, Liz and Mary, and they will have plenty more adventures soon!

If you would like to keep reading, the second book in the series, *The Invisible Woman,* is available to order now.

Acknowledgements

Thanks as usual to my husband, chief beta reader and long suffering sounding-board, Chris, for all your help in the writing of this book. Many thanks also go to my mother for traipsing around Stirling for several days at the Bloody Scotland festival which helped cement the direction and themes for this book.

The wonderful on-line community of the Bestseller Experiment and the BXP team deserve special mention for their support and in particular feedback on title and cover design. Extra thanks to Angela for very kind last minute beta reading.

And ultimate thanks go to the town of Paisley, for allowing me to ever-so-thinly disguise you as Invergryff in this novel. It may rain a lot, but the mums in the playground are the best around. Cheers!

Printed in Great Britain
by Amazon

19278525R00185